# THE STRANGERS

*Acknowledgements*

Thanks to the editors of the following publications where portions of this novel appeared in slightly different form: EXPLORING*fictions*, *The Brooklyn Rail*, *The Denver Quarterly*, and *Harp & Altar*. For their encouragement and support many thanks are given to Lynn Crawford, Alan Davies, Luca Dipierro, Corey Frost, Ning Li, Norman Lock, David McAleer, Keith Newton, Alex Samsky, Joanna Sondheim, Shannon Steneck, Jamil Thomas, Danny and Cassie Tunick, John Yau, and Leni Zumas.

# THE
# STRANGERS,

## CONCERNING THE

# *Moribund Language*

### OF

# OONA AND OON, the
# SPUKHAFTE FERNWIRKUNG
# of NOON and NOONA, and
# *THE MYSTERIOUS*
# LIBRARY-SHIP OF HENRY
# AND THE CAPTAIN:

DESCRIBING OBJECTS AND EVENTS FROM
TYPICAL LIVES OF ITS PERIOD AND PLACE

*and giving an account of how certain of its heroines, stand-up
artists, and filmmakers were deliver'd from tyranny,
abduction, and divorce.*

NEW YORK CITY   MMXIII   BLACK SQUARE EDITIONS

BSE BOOKS ARE
DISTRIBUTED BY SPD:
Small Press Distribution
1341 Seventh Street
Berkeley, California 94710

1-800-869-7553
orders@spdbooks.org
www.spdbooks.org

CONTRIBUTIONS TO
BSE CAN BE MADE TO:
Off The Park Press
73 Fifth Avenue
New York, New York 10003

(please specify your donation
is for Black Square Editions)

TO CONTACT THE PRESS, PLEASE WRITE:
Black Square Editions
1200 Broadway, Suite 3C
New York, New York 10001

An independent subsidiary of Off The Park Press

*for*

JOANNA SONDHEIM

Often I go out onto the street, and there I seem to be living in an altogether wild fairy tale. What a crush and a crowd, what rattlings and patterings! What shoutings, whizzings, and hummings! ...And one thinks of undreamed-of streets, invisible new regions, equally swarming with people... What is one, really, in this flood, in this various, never-ending river of people.

— ROBERT WALSER

Form does not differ from emptiness; emptiness does not differ from form.

— *The Heart Sutra*

# I. BROTHER

The owl is to the cat as the angel is to the man.
—CHRIS MARKER

A T NIGHT when I can't sleep and at noon in the streets I don't know who I am and could be anybody. Is it so uncommon? Glancing—a sideways look, head tilted—at your own peculiarities: the sins the beauty the beauty marks the children the parents the siblings the untold the told sufferings — couldn't they all be so easily swapped? For any of the faces in the crowd or the phantoms that pass through my bedroom or that lie with me on the bed or any of those spirits somewhere else in the house. I spin around and can't sleep. I'm a zombie in the street. The noon sun beats down.

Later on. But then what do we do with the facts? They pebble and loom and soil us up (but that's a prejudice; they're as clean as paper, as clean as us). They're stacked around us, very close. Here are mine: I'm sitting in my attic apartment looking out its round window, practicing my routine for tonight. It's about to rain, in fact it's beginning to. The radio announces "Terrible

terrible times!" and I click it off and put on a record of piano music and, passing to put the old one in a sleeve, look again onto the slickening street. A beautiful-looking woman walks fast. She needs an umbrella. Dark, wet spots on her blouse.

Over my desk is a painting of a ship. It sails through a ruffled blue and small colorful flags snap flat off its masts. My secretary bought it for me because she heard that having a painting of a ship over your bed would give you sweet dreams. It started out over the bed but now it's over the desk. (Someone said where it was "wasn't the right spot.") (In fact, my wife's the one who said that.) My secretary is kind to me. She is moody, older, has a son my age, is many years with the company. No one will fire her. She works at a snail's pace. In fact she doesn't do anything at all. I do everything myself — but don't mind. It's not very much work. People always complain but working hard is easy. I can do a day's work in an hour and the rest of the time chat with my secretary as she pretends to work. She has problems: her aunt is in the hospital; her husband's best friend is a drunk; the creditors are after her (she says this to me slyly, with a smile). But there are daily things to celebrate, she reminds me. Your handsome son! she says to me. I know I know, I say and take a sip of the wretched coffee she can't help but make poorly every day.

I have all kinds of friends. We smear each other's bodies in various rooms and are passers-by of each other's welfare. A society. I have a wife and son — though now they live across town, but that's not so unusual. At the club where I perform there's always someone to talk to. They all know me and if not there, there are other clubs and bars and theaters and galleries in which to duck in and out of shadows and also glaring or flattering lights to jump into and out of.

All the faces in the crowd or in the bed or around the table — and my own — are robots. Or animals — what's the difference. And maybe there was a family or a complete pleasure but now we're each helplessly marooned. That's me in a bad moment.

How funny it is to change moods. One morning I'm very energetic and chirping to the girls in the bakery and in the coffee shops, who seem either annoyed or happy to talk — but I can't really help myself in any case; it's so natural to talk talk talk when, after sleeping all night, I'm ready to go.

And then the very next morning — was it because of the last whiskey? the first one? — my mind wakes in recoil, doesn't want the eyes to open. The sore spots, which are everywhere especially behind the eyes, are tender and inflamed.

I WORK at a publishing company. We publish cookbooks and computer how-to manuals and poetry. Every two years we publish a self-help book. My secretary writes it. She doesn't know she writes it. I just listen and compile all her advice and publish it under the name Mary Cowell. They're bestsellers. They're very good. They say things like "Don't eat meat — or, not too much" and "The secret to life is to try your best" and "Forgive your friends" and "If you're angry breathe ten deep breaths" and "Say each day something nice to your spouse."

The cookbooks and computer manuals also sell well.

O N WORKDAYS in the mornings I put on a tie and a shirt. I try to match them and my socks stylishly. And once in a while someone at the office will say in my hearing that I'm a good dresser, but who can believe things like that. Still I try to choose carefully. Today's a Sunday though — and now it's raining.

I think about my routine a little, two or three things I want to include, then try to stop thinking about them — a method.

I wish I wish I wish.

L ET ME re-introduce myself. Before — it wasn't a lie but it was something to regret nonetheless. My name is Oon. I work at a publishing company and alternately spoil and take advantage of my elderly secretary. She returns the favor. Nights I do a stand-up routine at a club. A routine where I talk standing up.

I'm recently separated. Recent enough that at night I want to bound the chasm: tears remorse etcetera — but instead have been, am, sitting very still, like a bunny trying not to get devoured. Everyday problems, which hurt.

Mary Cowell's chapter titles are always questions. *Are you alive? Is it so important? What did my Nana mean when she said,* "You're borrowing trouble"? *Are you sure you want to win?*

I'm well-dressed but ugly. Warty, tubby, balding. A nose and eye-separation ill proportioned. Objectively ugly but nowadays I don't mind at all. In fact in combination with my dapper dressing I've evolved, in middle age, into the type people recall as *striking*.

So, then, from where this well of unwellness? That gets therapized and meditated and dieted as due my self-hating class?

I don't know, an indulgence, I haven't not thought many a time. Yet — it makes rotating through the days a heavy wheel. Grunt work. Who's asking for sympathy? Not me. It's not allowed. So I can only say I'm hoping to identify similar others so as to induce a later crisis: whether to then embrace or — take off.

ONE MORE TIME I think I'll get it right. If not it can't be said I didn't try. However, not much can't be said. My name's Oon. I'm in my apartment in the middle of a heavy summer storm. Big fat drops, sheets of rain. I open the window (not the round one which doesn't open but the one in the back) and let the cool breeze in and watch the rain lasers explode on the sill. The floor is getting wet but nothing bad will happen.

I work at a company. I love my secretary who is old enough to be my mother because she is old enough to be my mother. Other details like before but packaged in smooth round globes or sharp-edged crystal cubes.

I am recently separated from my wife. Together we have a young son.

I'm due at the club in a few hours and so should think about what to wear.

I go stand by the closet and recall how we met.

ONE NIGHT about fifteen years ago I was doing my stand-up act. I was talking standing up. I was talking about women. I made some generalizations about them. I said, "Women's musculature makes them inferior badminton players." My punch-line was traditional: "Shuttlecock." Or I might have said, "Women live on average ten years longer than men." Pause. "In developed nations." Or maybe I said, "The owl is to the cat as the angel is to the woman."

Someone stood up in the audience. I could only see her out-line from the light-drenched stage. "That's it," she said. "That's enough. I, I, I can't take this. Anymore. That's right. You don't know what you're talking about. The notion of reality you depict is worse than shoddy — it's mistaken."

A heckler.

I was a professional (or at least a hard-working amateur). I'd known hecklers. Sometimes, as practice and as philosophical exercise, I would even heckle. I'd go to friends' and strangers' shows and fire a volley. My aim was true but mostly I'd get the overwhelming response. The heckler is after all at the disadvan-tage, always on lower ground.

So in this case I wasn't sure if she was a heckler of the practic-ing or actually enraged variety. In either case I was compassion-ate. To deny or defy speech is an honorable occupation. But my role is prescribed nonetheless. I've to crush.

"Where are you from?" I asked the heckler.

"Farther than you," she said, defiant. And added, "And from deeper down too."

"Ha — a nationalist! What a wimp!" The crowd chuckled, already behind me.

"You and what army." Her deadpan was dangerously plump,

ripe. I felt the audience, so recently on my side, teetering. My pits dampened.

"How about the squad behind you?" I gambled but was startled when she then rushed the stage. When she was almost upon me I reflexively defended myself (so I thought) by bonking her on the head with the microphone.

"Brute!" she cried and swiveled and grabbed my beard with one hand and my nuts with the other. "I've your tokens of manhood now!"

I ran my tongue quickly around the channel of her outer ear. That got her riled and I saw suddenly that I was in over my head. I made a quick decision, feinted left, then right, then jumped off the stage and banged out the nightclub door and into my car, shoved it into gear and squealed off.

Unluckily she too was well-parked.

We raced down the main drag and then onto the highway. My phone rang and I picked up. It was her! (My rear window had a sign: "Make offer.")

"Hey shit-for-brains," she started, "you're nothing but a skewed journalist. You know." She waited for effect. "Garbage in, garbage out."

That stung. There was no audience now, which elevated it. What we were engaged in was a matter of honor. "Oh yeah?" I said.

"Yeah," she said.

I fiddled with the radio for five minutes.

Then I said, "Your mom and dad were virgins."

That must have done it. She sped up to come alongside me and slammed her car into mine, sandwiching me against the railing. We spun out. Her car, a svelte compact, rolled over twice. Mine, a late model sob, popped over a cement divider and fell like a whale diving, upside-down with a glassy crunch. Both vehicles settled in spark and smoke on one of the manicured lawns within a highway cloverleaf. We realized simultaneously that we'd reverted to hack TV moves and, mostly out of shame, jumped out of our respective cars for the final round. I remember having the thought, "If I'm going to go down I'm doing so on my own terms."

"Your environmental concerns are pure self aggrandizing!" she spit out.

"Cynicism which betrays arrested development," I squawked back.

"You're a cat lady with too many shoes!"

"Dipskull!"

"Numbshit!"

We stopped a foot apart, tense. She threw me down and we immediately began to make love very slowly and gently and anally.

It was pretty much at first sight.

SOMETIMES, DURING one of my frequent bouts of insomnia, I daydream, I pretend, that I've a twin. Which is strange, almost hilarious, because I do have a twin, my sister. But I daydream I pretend of a different twin, an identical twin, another me living a not-so-dissimilar existence but twenty blocks away, but for whom life has destined a path never to cross with mine.

I'm in front of my closet, still choosing for tonight. There is the T-shirt with the cute-but-fierce bird, there is the rather sophisticated striped one, and there's a melon-colored collared shirt with dark lavender stitching. Sometimes it's effortless. Sometimes it takes a long time of testing. Part of it is being dazzled by the risk of failure.

Why did I make up that story of how we met?

As if I was at the club doing a routine. It's something when we tell stories to ourselves. And the *real* story of how I met my wife is actually very interesting. I turned around and she was there and I was *drawn* to her. We started talking and, while listening to her very intently, simultaneously I wasn't listening at all but measuring how my heartbeat was louder and my lungs seemed to have sunk into my stomach and how my penis was tingling as if about to leak. The body bypasses the brain and signals to itself with wild misfiring and its locomotives leap off the rails and with cogs seizing up. On the other hand maybe I was being poetic because it *was* like a movie car chase ending in a metal-twisting crash and with momentarily elaborate fucking.

It's terrifying that kind of love but I don't worship it. No longer anyway. Only the talented get that visitation often — and even then each time a fading. Maybe I'm generalizing more than I should, but I've a feeling I'm right. Anyway, now I'm more infatuated with the achievements, both potential ones and past ones, hanging in my wardrobe. (But even so I solemnly suspect this excess interest in fashion is only a distraction. Who cares though. Or, who has a choice?)

How did I become so airy today? Let's eat something so we don't think ourselves priests. You never think of priests eating baloney sandwiches smothered with mayonnaise, do you?

A sweet pickle finger-dug out of the jar to perfect the argument. Crunch crunch.

NOTHING IN my closet seems right so I decide to take the afternoon, even though it's raining, and go shopping for a shirt. Maybe I'll find it maybe I won't. These days, I like to be completely taken up with frivolous adventures — of course in dead seriousness, in absolute earnestness, with perhaps some conception of an underlying frivolousness, but with a dead seriousness nonetheless. Would you believe, you probably would, but would you believe that not that long ago, not so long ago, this kind of adventure would be unthinkable to me? Before, I wore the shirts I owned and didn't think of them one way or another and ate only beans and rice, all kinds of beans and all kinds of rice — red beans with brown rice and brown beans with white rice and white beans with black rice. I got on in a dull, plodding, serious way... And then? And then I met alcohol and it loosened me right up!

Not immediately of course, not exactly like a magic elixir, but, yes, as with a kind of potion, I was slowly transformed from one being into the next. I don't think it had to be alcohol. It could have been ballet. Something like that. Getting completely taken up with something like ballet. Or I could have moved. From New York to Moscow. Or to Kansas City. Or from the Lower East Side to Rego Park. Any of that could have done it — and maybe it was, who knows, just getting up each morning.

But the potion — let's say it was that — slowly, in *human* time, worked its magic.

And it was around this time I made it a point to become a stand-up artist. Someone who talks standing up. I was already working at the publishing company. (My secretary was already old.) At that time I was still in charge of the history books and the poetry books. Our self-help books were already blockbusters. But I was constantly terrified and thought myself valiant. The thing I drummed into myself and my friends was: Vigilance!

But then one day I went (reluctantly) with some friends to a club.

It was called The Library, which was odd because the interior had a nautical theme. When I think of nautically themed restaurants I think of kitsch, but this was rather a refined place. Thick sections of rope were chopped up and hung on the wall almost angrily — the smell of it, the musk of the rope, perfumed the air. The furniture and detailing were made of heavy dark wood, wet-looking due to a high burnish.

I didn't think I'd enjoyed myself, at least not profoundly, but I found myself returning there, often alone, to drink at the bar and watch the candlelight reflected in the wooden tabletops, to smell the hemp-y rope smell and to watch the stand-up artists.

I know why I'm telling you this story I think. But while I'm telling it, it may please you to know that I'm grabbing my keys and my wallet off the dresser and heading out to see if I can't find a good shirt for tonight. Oh, taking an umbrella too — it's still raining, now a very heavy summer rain.

One reason also I went so often to The Library was the food. It served an interesting menu, a kind of a goof of a menu. The cook was an understated conceptual artist — that's what I'd call him. He'd learned to cook in Nice and Barcelona and Hong Kong (at "all the best places," like they say) and had had a dream, which he fulfilled at The Library, of opening a great vegetarian restaurant, one that was affordable and delicious and entirely vegetarian, except for — and this was the goof — it would have one meat option: a plain pan-fried hamburger with pickles and one thick ring of raw white onion slice, served with a mandatory small glass of dark beer. His name was Jeff.

I found myself going back to The Library time and time again until eventually I decided I wanted to do it too. I wanted to do a stand-up routine. I wanted to talk to a room standing up. So I did two things: I began to practice. I watched the seasoned and the novices and I emulated and rejected and, in my room, shadow boxed and shadow danced and shadow walked and shadow talked. The second thing I did was moonlight. I got a job as a waiter at The Library. I waited. I waited tables. I waited.

It was a good time, probably the best — better than later — to wait tables and listen to the routines and eat Jeff's food on my break. But it was painful also to be next to it and not do it, especially after I decided *to* do it, that is, after I decided to try it, so eventually — I had to do it. I had to practice, then audition, then do it. The whole thing was humiliating, each step — all of them repeated — and each step offered something humiliating, each step offered new and deep humiliation, *newer* and ever *deeper* humiliation, all along the way. I practiced and if I thought about doing it, in front of people, actually standing up, talking standing up, then I would become mortified. It was a soufflé of humiliation of mortification — like one of Jeff's desserts, something dusted with cinnamon — something dusted with ambition, painful and rich bites. It's raining so hard that walking through it even with the umbrella has soaked my cuffs. But I'm enjoying the rain, the choice to be walking in it. Likewise was the choice to try the stand-up, to try to talk standing up — all the humiliation and mortification was probably even the point in a way… After about a year and a half of this, of practicing my routines for Jeff and for my secretary and in front of the mirror, the day came when Jeff and my secretary and my mirror all said: go for it. And I approached the owner of The Library and asked him for an audition.

The material I was working on was obliquely political in nature.

There was a famous painter whose work I'd come to admire. He did these uncanny landscapes and portraits and for most of his career he was deemed unfashionable, somehow barking up the wrong tree compared to other more quote pyrotechnic or quote virtuosic or fashionably quote avant-garde artists. But then, somehow, the tide turned and his painting — which was of course virtuosic in its own way, pyrotechnic in its own way — became fashionable. Who knows how these things work, just that they happen the same way again and again and over again. So while most of his adult life this painter had lived cheaply, dirt cheap, out on the fringe or even literally, for a long time, for years, in squats, now, suddenly in old age he'd become wealthy.

To make a long story short, the wealth killed him.

It was a transported organ he rejected. It made him bloated, then green, then cancerous — and then he just popped, like a balloon.

But that's not exactly the tragedy of the story, or, only the first bit. His kids, after he died, started squabbling over the money. They're all drunks or in debt or just normally greedy and can smell the money, can feel its money-feeling against their skin. I knew this because I had just read in the paper that an auction house was going to have an exhibition — an exhibition for an upcoming auction. All this had been arranged by the greedy or debt-ridden or sodden or normal kids. An exhibition so that buyers from Japan and Luxembourg and Brazil and the like could see the wares before auction.

So that in a few rooms at the top of a skyscraper for a short time, you could see most of this painter's exquisite and mysterious landscapes, all together for the first — and last — time. Last, because after the auction of course, where these painting were to be sold to rich Japanese men and rich Japanese women, rich Luxembourgian men and rich Luxembourgian women, rich Brazilian men and rich Brazilian women, the paintings would of course then be crated up and sent to Japan and Luxembourg and Brazil to be hung over the desks and beds and staircases of these rich men and rich women from Japan and Luxembourg and Brazil and the like — *never to be seen again.*

On the one hand who cares. Beauty is everywhere and even if a good painter is a rare and long-suffering thing, from one perspective of course, that hardly matters. It's a kind of fortune just to be able to *see,* let alone be a good painter — and each act of fate is its own and only reward. There's that basic school of thinking and I'm not in disagreement with it. But. On the other hand: what a typical stupid tragedy!

My routine was about that, my stand-up routine, my routine where I talk standing up. Not so explicitly actually. It mentioned this story about the painter hardly at all really. Mostly I spoke of other things. Pinks in landscapes; raisins in salads; the idea that life is just one thing trying out different forms — an idea I'd had; or another similar idea: that everyone I meet is actually a version of myself, is myself, or that all the people together are also myself; brandy made from pears. But the heart of the routine, in my estimation, was the story of this landscape painter.

At least that was my opinion. I thought that all the stories were secretly heartbreak stories, stories somehow about work and disappointment and eventual and inevitable destruction — but that also the stories were linked, were locked, were constructed together — and the heart of them, the key to them, was this story about the painter. So I was more than a little surprised when the club owner, after I'd gone through my routine, when I was auditioning (nervous, sweaty, hopeful), I was surprised when the owner came up to the stage — no one else was in the club — and looked at me and said, "I liked it but the bit about the painter. Cut that out and you'll go on."

I didn't know what to say. I nodded and didn't speak, but I didn't know how to do it without the painter story. It didn't make any sense and I couldn't flow from one part of my routine to another without the painter story. In the end I just did it with the painter story. I lied. I said I wasn't going to do it with the painter story and then, that first night, I just did it with the painter story. The owner complained a little, but really not much, and I said I couldn't figure out how to do it without the painter story and he just shrugged and let it go and I went on.

I'M ON THE STREET with all the cute shops. There's a reason, it may even be obvious, why all the shops that sell restaurant furniture end up on one street and why all the shops that sell Indian food similarly on one street, and similarly ladies shoes and knockoff perfumes and diamonds and men's shirts — but no gathering on one street of shops that sell potted plants or maternity wear or ceiling fans or prosthetics. To explain market economics a professor once asked his students, Who feeds Paris? It was an economics class but I think it's a religious question. On this street are several shirt-shops I like. Designed in Berlin and London and Los Angeles but sewn in Sao Paulo and New Delhi and Guangzhou. City names like pearls on a string. Ulan Bator, Hanoi, Dhaka, Detroit, Islamabad, St. Petersburg, Athens, New York. This one has a very handsome window display so I walk in. Youthful shirts with winking logos or carefully absented logos. In that commercial din sometimes a beautiful idea.

I did the routine — the one pointedly *with* the painter's story — every night for two weeks. On the second to last night, after I'd finished, I was drinking an Old Fashioned at the bar with Jeff. I was watching someone else's act — a somber one involving spider webs and more to the point: death — when a woman approached.

She said, "Your act was likeable but for its hesitations."

I paused and looked up. "Stuttering is natural. When someone is overly fluent I can't trust them."

"B-b-b-but," she said.

I smiled and gestured to an empty seat.

She said, "I can tell you're Korean."

"Thank you," I said.

"You know what I mean. I am one too. Not a native-born. I was born here. Am I assuming too much?"

"No."

"You can tell me what you think," she said. "I was until recently a systems engineer — do you know what that is? I'm not sure myself. What is being engineered? Systems. This isn't a semantics game but is just another aspect of the problem I'm trying to tell you about. Systemsssss. Plural. Ambiguity multiplied to an absolute. You're still listening. Thank god. I've tried to say this over and over. But maybe you're just patient, maybe you're not considering what I'm saying at all, and are just nodding warmly as to a friend who has ended up in the loony bin and to whom you're obliged to spend a visiting hour with. But I'll continue trustingly.

"You can see I'm not rushing, I'm not screaming, spittled. I don't have that mad look in the eyes — I hope you don't see that mad look in the eyes. You can't see it. It's not there. There's no mad look in the eyes. This is not unthought out. I was a systems engineer.

"Plucked out of college, groomed from birth to be a calculating machine — so many of us were like this, trained to find the most logical conclusion. First, to be efficient. Then to minimize risk and to seek the long-term goal unremittingly, and finally to maximize reward. In our parlance: to monetize. I'm thirty-five now. From the time I was a sexually active being, before, from early pubescence, they've had me doing this. They is me. They are what I now am. They are what you now are. There aren't any exceptions. Each of us more grist for the mill. Is this starting to sound like something you've heard before? It isn't. It's only what you're always hearing, just that. The sound of structures built upon themselves. Creak.

"I thank you for not showing yet signs of boredom, for hearing me out. I wanted to tell you this. Frankly I wanted to tell this to *anyone*. But after hearing you I thought particularly you might listen, might understand. They assigned me to projects. I aggregated data, I interpolated, I assigned variables, I ran simulations, I defied chaos or accepted it and tried to learn from it and to work with it. But I didn't know how my piece fit into the whole, or I only had faith that it did, or I received a vague but inspiring vision from my bosses. Clouds, nets, leaves and rhizomes, cells. Tea dregs, stars, dominoes, palms, deck of cards. The problem was always scalability and thus a complete loss of proportion was manifest. When I was born a large room could hold twenty thousand volumes — and if you were diligent you would read half of them. Now the stores and annexes of Alexandria and Babel fit into my pocket and I'm so astonished I don't read a thing. I was born into a town of several thousand and because it was clear my family and I were outcasts, I knew who I was. Now I live in this city of millions and I'm sure that everyone I see is myself and that I'm a drunk glass of water. Am I being bombastic, absurd? I ran from the company with secrets. I can't possibly profit from them. Even the ideas are laced with codes that bear trademarks. I don't even know what the secrets *are* — just that I have them because of the agents and assassins they send. I'm not so impor-tant — it's just protocol, procedure. Agents to convince me to return, assassins if I refuse. Sometimes they're one and the same. The latest is an Egyptian sitting over there named Mu'nisah who has a reasonable, undeniable voice and, in her handbag, a needle full of poison. Go ahead turn and wave. No don't. Why give her the satisfaction. Thank god you're still listening, not trying to fob me off. I want to be heard tonight, to have you listen. Every-thing I've done I'm repudiating but it's impossible to defy.

"I've tried to trick them by behaving exactly as I was supposed to or rebelling outright or alternating the two — they didn't care. Death itself will be a single digit used to trigger another event, a notch in a sequence mindlessly anticipated — if such a thing is possible. To plan and carry out a giant complexity but without will, without mind, without comprehension — is such a thing possible? History itself. Time itself. Systemssss. What could I do? Wasn't there a joke I could tell? A list of friends' names to recite? The worst of it is is that the device I helped build is not a doomsday device — just an evolving set of humdrum enslavements. Thank god you're listening, digesting each word it even seems — so I'll come out and ask it, to move the plot along. You are listening, right? Ok, here is it. From the agent-assassin, will you do the right thing? Will you help me?"

I'D HEARD everything but hadn't really retained it since, while she was speaking, I'd ordered and consumed several pear brandies. She was very beautiful and so I was nervous. Her sincerity was touching and I thought if I played my cards right I could maybe have a thing with her. I glanced into the mirror to see Mu'nisah, her agent-assassin, and noted that my companion was right — the Egyptian was there: menacing, portly, and cruel-eyed with an elegant lavender dress that somehow revealed luxuriously-cared-for skin. I said, "Would you like to see some paintings?"

"How can we? It's past midnight," she said.

"Then come with me. We'll walk to my house. And tomorrow we'll go see them."

"The paintings you spoke of? The ones to be sold?"

"Yes."

"Okay."

We got up. We were both wobbly from drink, which I was grateful for as the alcohol had made her paranoia attractive. I was hoping the same could be said of myself.

OUTSIDE the night air and the still teeming streets began instantly within us the painful process of becoming sober. We felt the chemical leave our cells, a sponge drying. As we were walking I did not dream of her naked or of our bodies in relief but instead could not shake the vision of Mu'nisah sneaking up behind me to plunge a needle into the vein of my neck. And as she did so I also saw her face, her eyes and her smile — all conveying a perfect reasonableness, almost a friendliness, dispensing poison as if a friend had been fishing for a compliment, and she was politely, readily obliging.

I shuddered and blamed exhaustion and then thought I'd paid too close attention to my new friend's story. I tried to picture her naked instead and in doing so, blurted out the question, "What's your name?"

"Gerta."

We continued walking.

BACK at my apartment, as we undressed, I again saw Mu'nisah's face in the vanity mirror. But, swiping, swerving, she wasn't there — an anti-vampire. Gerta, in panties and bra, from across the room: "What? What is it?"

"Gnat," I replied.

"Huh?"

"I mean. Um. Spider web, thread. You ready?"

She pointed a finger at me. I pointed one back.

We crossed the room, led by our pointing fingers, aiming them sloppily at one another until our fingertips met in unreasonably shy stiffness.

IT WAS then gotten over quickly enough, but even so, while on my back and with Gerta over me and in my hands, I saw Mu'nisah again. She was looming over us both and her expression was one of mild pity.

My eyes widened in horror, which Gerta interpreted as a culmination of purpose and so began to gyrate even faster. I closed my eyes then and thus made her interpretation true.

THE NEXT morning Gerta and I stood before a skyscraper, chilled by its shadow, not looking up its impossible and obscene face, inside the top of which were displayed the temporarily gathered paintings.

Our brief fascination with each other may have clicked dead, for me, in the express elevator. As our motion accelerated and the counter above the doors read, "xx," a tombstone, and even though we were alone, I couldn't bring myself to think of her. She already wasn't even a distraction. I was thinking instead for some reason about Mu'nisah and her needle of poison and was therefore surprised and not a little horrified when the elevator doors opened to reveal her standing before us.

Gerta and I got off while Mu'nisah squeezed past us and took the elevator back down.

Gerta answered my look, saying, "I told you so."

"I know," I said, "but doesn't it ever scare you?"

"There's only so much you can do, and besides, I don't think they're after me anymore."

"Why not?"

"I think last night when we touched fingers I transferred their proprietary files to you."

"When we touched fingers?"

"A euphemism for fucking."

"Files?"

"Another euphemism."

I was going to respond but, catching sight of the paintings we'd come to see, whatever thought I'd had suddenly seemed unimportant. The morning crowd circulated around the paintings. Mostly they were landscapes, the palette heavy with muddy browns and an occasional, destructive pink. Half a dozen portraits showed wealthy-looking men and women staring out of the canvases, their eyes filled with the most palpable shock.

I loved these paintings immediately and so much I forgot everything but looking — a greedy, insatiable sucking in of sight. I didn't believe what I was seeing.

But after an hour or two I began to calm down and the paintings began to flicker between some cosmic world and this mundane one. I was then able to speak.

"Do you like them?" I asked Gerta.

"A little clever," she said.

"Hm," I said.

"I think we pretend ecstasies more than we feel them."

"Why would we do that?"

"The heroism of the ecstasy-seeker's gamble."

"Is it false?"

"It's temporary."

We wandered the floor one more time. "What now?" I said.

"We have to destroy a painting."

"Huh?"

"Isn't that what we've been discussing?" she said. "Isn't that why we're here? This moment of collection is only possible because of base mechanisms. But of course those base mechanics who have made such an event possible would never recognize their baseness. Even what I'm about to do, which is only to hold up a mirror to their own acts, will be dismissed as a singular derangement. Its symbolism will be too concrete to map onto the greater destruction of their abstract commerce. It will do nothing but it will be what we'll do."

"You're loony."

"Pick the painting."

"Nope."

"Pick it."

"No."

"Pick."

"Not gonna happen."

"Pick it."

I looked around. My favorite was a shallow landscape of an iridescent riverbank. In it, there was a small figure yelling from the far bank and a police cruiser flashing its lights. It was a moment of crime conflated with the history of painting and with nature.

"That one," I said and walked away from her.

She began a minute later, quietly, without screaming. She lifted the canvas off the wall and punched her hand through its center. She snapped the frame over her knee, folded it, and then stomped on it. She produced a small can of black paint from I don't know where and was pouring it over the heap of mangled frame when the security guards finally came and yanked her away from the thoroughly destroyed painting. It was only then that she began screaming. She cursed them, a torrent of repeating obscenities. She screamed, "You motherfucking fuckers," and she kept repeating it. They stuffed her kicking and flailing and screaming into the express elevator and you could hear her muffled curse for a long time until it finally faded. A hysteria and a mad righteousness. You fuckers. *You motherfucking fuckers.*

I was waiting for someone to approach me, ask me a question, but nobody did. I decided to leave, but just as I was about to, Mu'nisah appeared.

"Hello, my name is Mu'nisah," she said.

I said hello and we shook hands. This was when I first touched the person who would become my wife.

A T THAT MOMENT, even though just a short while previously I'd been dreaming of Mu'nisah's assassinating tendencies, I was oddly very drawn to her. She still had the same cruel eyes, but she was dressed in a beautiful suit with an open, high-collared white shirt. Though she looked like a squat, wealthy cross-dresser, the effect was somehow more glamorous than comic. "I'd love to buy you a coffee," I blurted out.

She smiled as if it were a very natural offer and led me by the hand, which she hadn't — or I hadn't — let fall. In the express elevator, as our motion downward accelerated, I felt my fascination with Mu'nisah pulse and engorge like a sexual organ, and the "xx" in the counter above the doors were now the eyes of some pagan god, under which we were taking silent, carnal and sacred vows.

This is the mood I was in when the doors slid open to let in cold, conditioned air and which allowed us a view of a small man-made waterfall at the center of the skyscraper's lobby.

"A stranger's hand and chaste, modern sex in the express elevator of Hotel Utopia, our first marriage," I thought to myself, typically eager, unusually correct.

"THERE's a restaurant over there," she said, leading. It turned out to be a book-lined café called The Ship, which was odd as it had no accoutrements to go with this sea-faring title. With floor-to-ceiling bookshelves and a quiet, scholarly-looking wait-staff, it more resembled a library. The food however was excellent. I had a rich mushroom fagioli soup and a beautiful piece of bread with fresh hummus. The coffee too was bittersweet and strong. Mu'nisah had a hamburger and a small glass of dark beer.

We didn't talk while we ate, but after the dishes were cleared Mu'nisah broke the silence and said, "I'm not suffering but I'm only waiting to die. It's been a short, full life." She paused. I felt her wanting me to nod, to encourage her on, though I was a little fearful to do so. I finally said, "What makes you so sad?"

"I'm not sad. Like I said, relatively speaking, I don't suffer. Initially, when I was very young, I was an intellectual and a communist. I felt everything could be shared and that poverty was an abomination. Later, because of painful experiences, betrayals — I betrayed and was betrayed — I had to admit that my revolutionary fervor was untenable. Worse, I had to admit that my understanding of human possibility was both grandiose and simplistic. At that point I felt I'd realized my fate, that the understandings left for me had been achieved. A mysterious feeling, I felt unmoored and completely devoid of potential."

I said, "Maybe you can be more concrete. Where did these things take place? I'd heard you come from —"

Mu'nisah slammed her hands on the table making me jump. "What's it matter!"

With that gesture she made me realize again the uselessness of certain puffed-up facts. She seemed to be saying that if I didn't pay attention to her breathing shape and her utterances, I'd just be repeating all the mistakes that were so common and yet so difficult to avoid. "Please go on," I said.

"Not that long ago I caught sight of a distant hope. Some other idea shone on the horizon and I felt myself moving toward it, gathering velocity and courage. I came to believe in the profit motive and in the limited compulsions of our race and in the efficient distributive forces of capitalism. Infinitely complicated universes were built premised on clear and simple rules. How glad I was to be becoming realistic! But then my father — or someone who looked very much like my father — went into politics and needed a good aide, a reliable secretary. I joined him and for several years we enacted important laws. But then I became corrupted as did this man I worked for. He killed himself in the large house in which he'd lived alone. I ran away and changed my name, the first of several times. I may have imagined my pursuers. I think the uncertainty of their existence was part of their method of revenge. Eventually — it didn't take long really — the empty feeling, the feeling that the finality of my knowledge had been reached, returned. In fact it was more set, more intractable, because I realized I had tried to delude myself that this ultimate stage had not yet been reached, had deluded myself into thinking more was available, and now had to face very bitterly that I'd tricked myself, and in fact had debased the trivial but only important thing I owned — that is, some sense of the truth — out of weakness, out of pernicious boredom, out of a disgusting desire for entertainment." She let this final accusation hover, opened her mouth as if she wanted to begin again, but then closed it and looked out the window. After a while, I gathered that she was finished.

I COULDN'T HELP but take Mu'nisah seriously — she was a very serious person. Nonetheless, despite her seriousness, I suspected her convictions weren't as steadfast, her conclusions not as final, as she presented them. I think it was this uncertainty, this suspicion, that made me decide to pursue her.

We got up and she invited me to walk her to her next appointment. My plan for the afternoon involved walking aimlessly around the bombed-out parts of the city so I agreed. It was a lovely day.

As we walked I asked her, "So what do you do now? For a living?"

She said, "I'm an economist at a think tank specializing in risk assessment for investments in unstable nations. How about you?"

I decided to lie. "I'm a biological engineer isolating the sterility code in the genome of crop plants so so-called third world farmers will be forced to re-purchase seed regularly." I was afraid she'd think I was sentimental if I told her the truth, but she saw through me.

"Don't lie. Your wardrobe is too stylish for that!" I wanted to rebuke her, but just then it appeared a bum was approaching us to panhandle. Mu'nisah and I prepared to shoo him away, but then I recognized that in fact it was Brian, one of my best friends. I introduced him to Mu'nisah who said hello and then that she was leaving us as she had to make her next appointment.

"Can I see you again?" I asked.

"I have to consult my spiritual advisor," she said.

"Who's that?"

"Actually he's my former husband, but he's very advanced and I always consult him before dating anyone."

"Okay," I said and gave her my phone number. She waved goodbye and Brian and I set out in a different direction.

It's still raining and I'm in another of those cute shops thinking about buying a flashy suit. It would take guts but might be the piece of theatricality I need for tonight's show. It's summer and the suit is very fine and classic except for its bold color. I hold it up to myself and see myself in the mirror and then turn to look out into the street where people are rushing by under umbrellas and with determined looks and the street is shiny and bursting, alive and rippling, with the heavy rain.

It's sad but bittersweet to think of Mu'nisah and me in those first days. She was haughty and I was brave but a little in awe of her. After she'd left us I told Brian that I was fascinated.

"With her? She seems of the class we usually ridicule."

"I know," I said, "but I think her gaucheries might reveal un-tapped perversions."

"I admire your openness. And your work ethic," Brian said with a wide smile, but then his face fell a little and he said, "But I've some problems I wanted to discuss with you."

"Shoot."

"My mother is very sick and I just put her in the hospital but she'll be out soon and I don't have any money to take care of her. A visiting nurse is so expensive and I can't do it on my own. Also, and more importantly, my mother who was always difficult now knifes into my every fault. She keeps saying I'm a failure as a painter, a pretentious hack and that I stick to my dishwash-ing because I'm too scared to try to get a real job. I just want to run away, or for her to die even, or even to get a quote real job and make money and give up painting and just live next to her, wealthy, but with a destroyed look on my face — but that's just an unrealistic fantasy. The more realistic fantasy is that of her finally dead, but when I actually think of that one, carefully con-front its reality, I feel hopeless, defeated and crushed."

I turned to look at Brian's darkened face. I said, "Yes, but do you think Mu'nisah will call me?"

The full, green trees shimmered around us. The sun was warm on our faces and lit up the dusty, now golden path. We walked in silence for a little while more.

"Will you show me what you've been working on?" I then asked. Brian tucked a strand of greasy hair behind his ear and smiled. He nodded and we turned to walk out of the park toward his nearby apartment.

BRIAN's apartment was in its typical filthy state. I often lie
to myself and say I take pains to accept coarse reality, but
Brian's apartment would always force me to admit my hypocrisy.
That is: I don't know how he lived like that. His canvases were
either brutally nailed to the walls or crudely stacked – but these
were the only items in the place even roughly organized with
care. Grimy plates and cups were scattered everywhere along
with bits of food crumbled between the floorboards and on the
ancient rugs and smeared on the couch he also slept on. His
eccentric collection of clothes occupied four overflowing trash
bags. Piles of pornographic magazines mixed together with
tomes of philosophy and thick art books on European masters.
Globs of oil paint or perhaps dried cat vomit splattered every
inch of the floor. His mangy cat appeared as we entered, seemingly as devastated as his surroundings, to rub his patchy gray
fur against our legs.

"I cleaned up for you," Brian said.

"I noticed," I said.

I surrendered and flopped onto the couch. For an hour Brian brought out paintings for me to look at. We didn't talk much. There was a channeled but dumb rage in Brian's work that occasionally made a very good painting, but my opinion was that he was at best an uneven artist. Sometimes, because I had a little bit more money, I condescended to be his patron, but while I think he considered these transactions as having some kind of odd glamour, they inevitably left me feeling cheated. Today was different though, and maybe it was because of days like it that I continued the friendship.

"Wait, bring me that one," I said, gesturing to a canvas on his make-shift easel. Brian smiled.

"I just finished it. It's still wet," he said, swinging the painting down in front of me.

It was a political painting. Even though Brian was as politically naive as every other painter I knew, he could oddly, occasionally, pull one of these off, perhaps because of his natural talent at rage. The painting had two figures, one on his knees, the other in military garb standing behind him. Brian titled it bluntly: "It's called *Torture*," he said. The crude earthy mustards, the green fatigues, the rust-colored blood all were clear even while the edges of faces and limbs had been crushed or blurred by the painter. It was a fine picture. I thought my sister might like it.

We quickly settled on a price. "Let's celebrate," Brian said.

Brian put a lot of ice in the glasses, and we took our time sipping.

I asked him what he'd been thinking about when he'd painted the painting.

"Don't laugh, but all my ex-girlfriends. Stalin and Cheney; the Stasi and the Janjaweed. But also how cruel I'd been to this one or how that one had repeatedly shown me I was a coward or how this last one and I lingered on and on in a self-punishing trance. Being strung up, made to kneel in putrid water for days, not eating, forced to eat, African prisons, American prisons. Arguing about who paid for what, how to do the laundry, how to make the bed, how phony and hypocritical we each were and how we each just wanted to hurt each other." He paused and then he said, "That conflation led to an insight. I began to think about myself. With each painting it's like that. I start off with some remote idea, some paradox or dichotomy I think I'm struggling to resolve, but then as a solution appears or doesn't appear, as I struggle, I end up thinking about myself, some self-criticism or some facet I love or hate about myself, or some self-deemed heroism or crime. Each act of painting generated by this sun of egotism... But it's at that point that I start looking around me and seeing what else is there. That's when I notice my surroundings and the details in other's faces and clothes. I'm a painter so I see them well enough, or at least I think I do—but it's only after this process, when the sun finally collapses, when my strength is used up, that I can really finally see."

I shook my head. After a moment I said, "No. You're holding out on me. Don't be frightened. Tell me the truth."

Brian's mouth made a silent little laugh and then he said, "Maybe I'm scared to tell you... Two weeks prior I was coming home late. Maybe I was drunk, but I don't think so. I came into the apartment building and, he, well he must have been hiding because as soon as I unlocked the door I was shoved from behind. I fell face first into the hallway. I twisted and saw my attacker – just a kid but a face set to kill and he had a long blade in his hand. I started crawling backwards and then up the stairs, still crawling backwards. He said, 'Give me your money,' I pulled out my wallet and showed him it was empty. This enraged him… I yelled for help but no one was home or no one came. He took a swipe. I tried to scramble up but he caught my foot. He went through the top of the shoe, but see, it didn't go very deep. He ran out finally. I just crawled up here and locked the door and downed a big glass of vodka and passed out. In the morning it was fine. My sock was bloody but I cleaned it and wrapped it and it will be fine. No, look. It's almost all better already. Don't fuss… And the next day I started to work on that painting."

WHEN, LATER, I told Mu'nisah about Brian's answer she told me another story. "I'd just gotten off work," she said, "and was passing through a big plaza. A crowd had gathered around a boy. He was in his twenties. He was wearing a superhero costume – red and blue, a cape, the whole getup. He was doing a performance of a kind. He was shouting, "Freedom!" and "Don't pay your income tax!" and "Save the libraries! Empty the prisons!" You know, that kind of thing. And he'd accompany this shouting with these staggered leaps, attempts at or portrayals of flight. It was kind of comical but also aggressive and out-of-control.

I just walked by. But then people started rushing past me towards him. Someone said, 'The cops are arresting Superman!' I turned back and could see three or four had tackled him. By now a crowd had developed. He was really putting up a fight. He was a skinny kid and he wasn't hitting back but squirming fiercely and yelling, actually squealing like a small child in an utterly pathetic squeal: 'Get off of me! Pleeeease.' It was how he drew out that 'please,' a submissive whine and an absolute begging. All the while, squirming and pushing and twisting. The cops then gave him several hard punches to the side – it was shocking to see such physicality face to face – and he finally crumpled into a resigned splay of limbs. More and more he resembled a child. The people watching this were giggling. Maybe it was the costume, the absurdity of it what made them laugh. Eventually they picked him up. He allowed himself to rise slowly then, now a superhero again, no longer a child. As they took him away he transformed a final time and became animated again. He began yelling, 'For Freedom! For America! For Justice!' At that point I started laughing too, because he was still absurd but strong and unbowed."

I told Mu'nisah that she'd stumbled upon a real dream. She'd come across herself playacting a superbeing, a clownish but simultaneously truthful protestor, but one who was immediately found and crushed by the state – a performer whose fellow citizens could react to only with scorn and ridicule. But Mu'nisah disagreed.

"No, I was thinking about the cops," she said. "What it must have been like for them to so easily dispatch a superhero. I'm sure in that instant the shadow of disappointment passed over them."

THAT WAS with Mu'nisah later. With Brian I was quiet and just gazed at the ugly wound on his foot, breaking my silence finally by saying, "But do you think Mu'nisah will call me?"

"I guess," Brian said with a shrug, "it depends on what her spiritual advisor says."

AFTER A FEW more drinks I got up to leave. I told Brian I'd be by to pick up the painting in a couple of days. I was going to enjoy the soft, sweet effect of the afternoon alcohol by touring the bombed-out parts of the city, something I like to do as often as I can—but I was again interrupted.

My secretary called me. She said her toilet was backed up and was wondering if I could come by and fix it. I told her I'd be right over.

A SHORT WHILE later, standing in her bathroom, plunger in hand, looking at the muddy swirl and the rich clumps twisting in a yellow galaxy—I thought about the painting I'd just bought. And I remembered a story I'd heard about Braque, that he would often take his paintings into the woods in order to compare his work with Mother Nature's. When I'd told this to Brian he wryly remarked, "Another glutton for punishment."

I took the plunger and shoved hard several times, taking the backsplash philosophically, until I'd achieved my goal.

My secretary was waiting in her living room sipping from a can of beer. She went to her kitchen and brought out a can for me. I cracked it open and we sat together at her table. The beer was wonderfully cold.

A FEW DAYS LATER Mu'nisah called. Her spiritual advisor and ex-husband wanted to meet me. He was a tax attorney with an office on a seedy block. I arrived at the given address at the appointed time but had trouble finding the door to his office. Finally I saw a side entrance and went up two flights in a dark and crumbling stairwell. I went down hallways past other law offices, past literary agencies and ninety-nine cent stores, past hotel furniture show rooms and cell phone shops, past liquor distribution offices and commercial real estate brokers, until I finally saw a sign: Frank Exit, attorney-at-law and spiritual advisor. I knocked.

"Come in!" Frank said warmly. Immediately I didn't like him but suppressed the thought, smiled, and took his hand.

We sat across from each other over an ancient and battered coffee table.

He gave me an expectant look.

"Mu'nisah sent me," I prompted.

"Ah, you're the blue-balled prick."

"Excuse me?"

"Sit up son. Let me get a look. Sit up!"

I did my best.

"Tard's forehead. Bloodline's diminished then?"

"Sir?"

"No matter. Mu'nisah seems to have taken a liking."

"Yes," I said, "I think I like her too."

"Points for effort I'll give you that. Keep at it, keep at it, son. No need to give up yet."

"So?" I asked.

He coughed into his fist, looked out a non-existent window and then turned back to me. He said, "Okay, alright. Alright, okay. Buy low, sell high. But then you're stuck. Yes? How far out are you looking? What are the fundamentals. So called. Is there news? Is it priced in? Are you too late? Early? In other words: What's low? What's high?"

I shrugged.

"It's best you keep pondering that one hard, son, as it's central. But I'll throw some pearls before you piglet. Listen up. Always a borrower and lender be – if the rate is right. With great leverage comes great responsibility. Have an exit plan before you enter. Remember you can't win if you don't play. If you don't play, you can't lose. The money you put in the pot is no longer yours. When the trade turns against you – admit it. Buy before the breakout; sell into the herd. When you can't sleep at night, remember 'Greed is good,' and 'A rising tide lifts all ships — except the dumbfuck lazy ones.' Don't focus on the money, focus on the trade. What is risk? When the price is down and you're the most scared to buy, your risk is lowest. When the price is high and you're confident, your risk is greatest. Markets over-react to bad news, except when they don't. Be contrarian, except when they're right. It's not the despair, it's the hope that gets you. Even a dead cat will bounce. Big trees still don't grow to the sky. Catching a falling knife — takes skill. The market always wins. The other guy is training harder. And this above all things: to thine own risk management always be true."

"I don't mind being lonely at the top," I said.

"You're gonna get eaten alive," he said.

I WAS DISAPPOINTED and confused when I left, certain I'd given a poor impression, but a few days later to my surprise Mu'nisah called me. "Frank says you're okay," she said.

"He did? Um, great."

"He said you can't be as stupid as you look."

"What can I say — we hit it off."

"I'll pick you up at eight," she said, and hung up before I could respond.

I THINK I EXPECTED her to come in a limousine. At the very least in a foreign recent-model. But she arrived on a motor-cycle—a hog too. A real rumbler. The overall effect however isn't, I imagine, the intended one. Mu'nisah's short, plump figure astride that giant chrome machine looked rather like an over-ripe tomato with arms. She handed me a helmet and flicked her head for me to get on. When I did, she kicked free abruptly, forcing me to grab and then hang on for dear life to her fleshy waist. For a second we tottered dangerously before she opened up the throttle and we shot out into the summer's musky gloaming.

The wind caving around us made the world separate, just for ourselves. But this too was experienced in isolation so that eventually it was like everything else.

We snaked down the highway for a long while. And then for some reason she abruptly pulled off and turned into a fast-food restaurant's drive-thru. Without consulting me Mu'nisah ordered us a small bag of fries. We sat then on the curb of the restaurant's parking lot and passed the white paper sack between us.

"What were the twins names?" she said.

"Um, I'm not sure," I said.

"Ono and Nono?" she said.

"Non and Noo," I said, "Maybe."

"Noon and Noona," she said. "I'm pretty sure."

Before we'd stopped, I'd put my mouth next to her ear and murmured a magic story to her. I was sure she couldn't have heard me against the roar of the motorcycle. But somehow she had, or at least enough to ask about the main characters' names.

"Never mind," I said. "What do you want to do now?" The magic story I'd whispered to her was another heartbreak story I wanted to work into a routine: a twin searching for his sibling kills himself and his tormentor on the very vessel that is bringing him to reunification. But I wanted her to forget about that story, which was magic in that it was supposed to make her see me clearly and so fall in love with me. She wasn't supposed to know she'd heard it. To distract her I said, taking another French fry with fake confidence, "I went the other day to an animal shelter."

"You wanted to adopt an animal? A cat, a dog?"

"Not really... I like watching the shelter volunteers. Some of them are happy and strong but most have a brittle cheerfulness made even uglier by smugness. And what I like to do, what I'll do, is pretend to want to adopt the most pathetic animals, the most injured and most diseased, the infirm and gross. I play with the volunteers' emotions, pretending kindness, pretending interest, building up their expectations—because they really do love these flea bags and want to save them from the needle—but then dashing their hopes and saying that really I couldn't, after all, take in the animal."

Mu'nisah laughed. "You're lying," she said matter-of-factly. "You wanted an animal. Or maybe you began with that plan you mentioned, but then you were a victim. You had one idea and that turned into another. You surprisingly revealed to yourself that you, that you were—an animal lover!"

She was laughing at me, not vindictively at first, but as if discovering something endearing.

"No, that's not it at all. Or that's not what happened. I admit it's more complicated than I let on. In any case what happened is, what usually happens is, you're right, that I do find myself heartbroken and in love with the animal. But still I refuse myself. I go along with the joke just as I planned. I don't take the animal. Even if no one can find my joke funny any longer, certainly not me, still I play it out. Because someone in the past, myself, found the joke funny. I'm playing for an audience already gone and even when he was here—I mean myself, the myself who made the plan—he was only half-realized. Still, I'm loyal to him."

Mu'nisah blinked attentively.

"But the last time at the animal shelter the animals I saw were blind. Two blind cats, a little past kittenhood. Siblings, a brother and a sister. The animal shelter worker said they moved naturally, were in many ways indistinguishable from seeing cats, and it's true when I picked them up they seemed almost the same as the others. For some reason, these cats captured my heart most of all. What were their minds like! I imagined living with them and I kept taking them out of the cage one at a time, petting them until they purred, alternating between brother and sister... But because I felt committed to my joke, I insulted the woman showing me the cats. I did something vulgar so she had to ask me to leave."

"What did you do?"

"I lifted up my shirt and used my hands to frame one of my nipples and said 'I like to have cats lick me here.'"

"And that did it?"

"I told her I didn't think blind ones could be so trained.'"

Mu'nisah reached for a fry. I opened up the paper bag and said, "They're all gone."

She shrugged and withdrew her hand. "And that did it?" she asked again.

"Yes, the shelter worker gave me a puzzled look and then turned red. She knew I was making fun of her, which I had no longer wanted to do but felt a great compulsion to complete my task so critically embarrassed us both, and thus rejected the blind cats."

We were silent for several minutes. Mu'nisah took and folded the paper bag neatly into a flat square. We were on a date, our first, and I wasn't sure if it was going well. After a moment I smiled at her and took the flattened, folded paper bag from her lap and walked it to the trash can. "Shall we go?" I said.

We put on our helmets. She did a little tomato hop to start the bike and I got on. We made a gradual pan past the workers in the glowing service window as they spoke unheard words and made simple movements in their confined space. Mu'nisah followed the arrows of the drive-thru but took a route of slightly greater radius. And then after a brief pause at the edge of the lot, she vastly increased our speed to match that of the traffic on the perpendicular road, which we slotted into expertly.

Mu'NISAH DROVE US where the city met the water and down the concrete and synthetic coastline, finally stopping by the harbor. She got off and led me to the docks where a very large but somehow familiar-looking ship was moored.

"Do you recognize it?" Mu'nisah asked.

"Yes, but I can't quite place it."

"It's the one where your sister works."

"Ah ha! Yes, that's it. But. How do you know about that?"

"Your sister and I are good friends. She's never mentioned me?"

Embarrassed I had to admit, "The truth is my sister and I are no longer very close. We used to be. But since we moved to the city I hardly see her. For some reason we've begun to stay out of each other's way, as if we don't want to know too much about the other."

"I see," Mu'nisah said. "Well, your sister got permission for us to come on board tonight. You'll have to thank her next time you see her."

"Yes," I said, "I'll remember to do that."

WE HAD TO cross a complex network of gangways before we reached its berth. The vessel gleamed like a glacier rising out of the black waters. A smartly-dressed sailor greeted us.

"This is Oona's brother," Mu'nisah said.

"Oh, very nice to meet you," the sailor said. "My name's YJ." He had a pot belly and a sun-burnt, shaven head, but he filled out his whites rather handsomely. "I understand you'll be dining in the library."

"That's right," Mu'nisah replied, turning to me to explain, "Your sister arranged everything." YJ led us through the ship's interior, down into its belly. After about fifteen minutes of travel we arrived in the ship's library—a large place that seemed impossibly cavernous but with a cozy central reading room walled with dark teak bookshelves. There were comfortable-looking chairs scattered tastefully around in threes and fours. There were also reading tables, but the central one had been transformed, with the aid of candlesticks and a white cloth, into a dining table set for two.

As we circled the table I said, "Very impressive. Now, I'm beginning to remember. This ship is called *Flaming Creatures*, isn't it?"

"Of course!" said Mu'nisah. "You really don't talk much to your sister, do you?"

"It's been awhile," I admitted. I recalled that my sister had a unique job. She was the librarian on a special ship. It had various reputations – as an elaborate tax shelter; as a floating home for displaced dictators or, alternatively, for war refugees; as the world's greatest cineplex; but I'd heard it was for euthanasiasts, people who wanted to kill themselves or wanted help to kill themselves but weren't allowed, by the laws of their respective countries, to do so. The MS *Flaming Creatures*, so went the rumor I'd heard, was a luxury liner which took passengers out to international waters where a person's suicide fell under no particular jurisdiction and could therefore be committed with relative impunity. Needless to say the ship did a roaring business. Officially of course it was just an everyday cruise ship (though granted, a spectacularly well-equipped one), but people who needed to know about it could easily discover its clandestine purpose. Supposedly governments generally left its extra-legal activities unexamined. My sister and I had never discussed it.

YJ said, "Would you like a drink?"

Mu'nisah suggested YJ's specialty, a rye perfect Manhattan, which I happily agreed to, and we sat with them on two stuffed reading chairs across from each other.

"LET ME TELL you about someone I know," said Mu'nisah. "Just recently middle-aged, this man who works in a cubicle lives entirely in a dream of heroic actions where he bursts into rooms or struts down sidewalks or, actively, shoots back the always-best retort. But needless to say he is puffy and sad and barely knows how undeveloped he is, save a gnawing loneliness, which, though a widespread disease, is no less painful because it is common."

I answered, "The one I'm thinking of is the same age, fortyish. A bartender who has regularly risked security for fun her whole life, working—and working hard—for tips and free meals in restaurants and bars and cafés. She's dated beautiful and bright men, each good for a quick laugh but all of them in the end revealed to be a drifter or a loaf. However, these days even they are becoming harder to find. It matters to her that she's pretty, and though she still is, the only part of her girlishness to be preserved is a needy and alarming attempt at coyness, which she's yet to realize is pitiful. A good drinker and, despite all her hard knocks, one who will never say a mean word about anyone."

"A former boyfriend," said Mu'nisah, "who seemed such a bumbler and momma's boy, was surprisingly wonderful in bed. Not just athletic but clever and animal both, with a thrilling escalation of derring-do that went on for months. Outside of sex, his only seeming hobby was computer equipment, of which he was annoyingly and demonstratively expert."

I thought our date was turning for the better. "I had a girlfriend," I began, "who was a department store prodigal, who listened to clumsy four-four crooners and who furthermore smoked bodega cigars that made her breath stink—but who, with little effort on my part, would howl in shuddering, grateful orgasms and so made me feel unreasonably heroic. She broke up with me too, after seven years, citing terminal boredom."

"The drug fiends I've dated to the one have been disappointing."

"Same," I said, "yet each time I always start out with such oversized, romantic hopes."

"I fell in love with a sculptor," Mu'nisah said, "whose work was both delicate and cerebral, poor in materials but monolithic and, in the mind, indestructible once seen. Knowing the work, I met the artist through a friend of a friend of a friend at a party. Expecting a god, I found a pimply thirty-something who read only comic books and biographies of serial killers. I loved him even more because of the spectacular gulf between his exquisite work and his drab, familiar failings. His lovemaking, by the way, was the most furtive and ill-equipped. Yet if I showed you a work of his, you too would be convinced only an Akhmatova or a Mallarmé or a Sekhmet possible."

"I should say," I said, "that sex to me is as mysterious as disease and no program seems capable of guaranteeing outstanding success. I've had many sad, disappointing nights with elaborate costumes and special scents."

"Countless ones for me as well. Not to mention gray weekend trips built from the most pathetic hopes."

"Answering an advertisement," I said, "I met the perfect roommate. We started as roommates, then became best friends, then became lovers. He was the only man I've had sex with and I wouldn't say I'm particularly bisexual. The sex, while not great, was very comfortable and pleasant with him. We spent all our free time together and liked the same food and movies and books. We liked to play pick-up basketball games on the neighborhood courts and then would go for martinis afterward. I had to break up with him because I fell in love with a woman, and felt very guilty about it, but preferred the sex that way—and he soon after left the city. We never correspond, but I think of him all the time."

WE finished our drinks and YJ served dinner at the table. The food was surprisingly simple but good if bland: steamed tofu and vegetables with brown rice. However it was accompanied by a tasty Malbec. Dessert was a scoop of chocolate ice cream.

"This is the kind of meal I usually have at home," I said.

"Your sister said you might say that."

"She did?"

"I think she pays more attention to you than you realize. She loves you very much you know."

"She does?" I said.

I LOOKED AT Mu'nisah across from me over the transformed library table. I thought that her face didn't quite match her body, which I realized was the source of some of my confusion about her. At times she seemed a tall, angular person with the diction of a well-educated foreigner, with slightly and charmingly accented English. Other times she was chubby and with gruff, inarticulate language – and her foreignness then more like a sojourner, a migrant worker – and she was a little pitiful but also more threatening, a tough survivor who might be capable of slitting a throat or two, maybe my own. These were the caricatures I'd make for her, mirroring my sense of my own foreignness – as is often the case when immigrants meet – but these forms of her alternated and shifted and conflicted so she continued to be mysterious to me. The suspension of my final judgment of her was very satisfying and made me think, for some time, that she would be for me my life's only real passion. And even now I'm not sure if she was not or if she was.

I said, "Even though there appears to be so much variation, each of us operates with the hopes of achieving such similar goals— less or more complex based on our needs and circumstance and talents. We run or face a limited and profoundly repeating list of anxiety, incomprehensions, and terror. To understand this brings both a repulsion of this fact and a recognition of the ubiquity of our prison, as well as a profound sympathy and love for all one's fellow inmates, including ourselves, who are, it must be said, no better or worse off for having such an insight."

"Who hasn't thought the same," Mu'nisah rebuffed. "I'd rather talk about the weather, its just theoretical silence."

I felt myself beginning to sulk, but at that moment YJ came to offer us coffee.

"Maybe we could take a walk," I suggested. Turning to YJ I asked, "Could we explore the ship?"

"Of course," he said, "Feel free to look around, explore, and when you're ready, just send a pneumatic. There are tubes and stations in every room, clearly marked. And I'll come find you directly. By the way the captain also said she wouldn't mind a drink with you, should you be inclined."

"What an excellent idea," exclaimed Mu'nisah—even though I'd been thinking the very opposite. "Tell her we'll be there in an hour."

"Very good," said YJ, and began clearing our plates as we left.

Answering my look, Mu'nisah said, after we'd left the library, "The captain is a very interesting person. I don't think you'll regret it."

I nodded my consent though I wasn't convinced.

Mu'nisah had evidently been on the ship before and seemed to know her way around quite well. It was an enormous craft. She led me in a circuitous route, and I immediately became disoriented. If I was by myself it might have become a nightmare, one in which I sweatily tried to extricate myself out of the ship's maze. But as Mu'nisah was leading, I felt completely at ease. I had faith not that she would necessarily keep me safe, instead I only had faith that whatever Mu'nisah wanted to do with me, she would. But this simple, complete faith I found left me quite at ease.

She took me past the stage of a lush, velvety and gilded theater, through the pungent and humid air of a long hot house, under the chandeliers of an enormous ballroom, upon tiles where our shoes clacked next to green glowing swimming pools, beneath the giant screens of half a dozen small cinema rooms, and up and down several flights of encased spiraling staircases. The architecture of the ship was beyond my imagination — beyond, it felt, science.

While we were walking Mu'nisah told me the story of her first marriage.

"Do you mean Mr. Exit?"

"No, this wasn't Frank. This was my first husband. It was a very short marriage. Let me explain… It was when I was working for my father, or a man who so looked like my father I called him

Papá. He'd become a powerful man, a politician. In fact because I was his close aide, it could truthfully be said that we came to power together. We were a good team and in fact in the beginning were trying to be helpful, to be civically useful. It's possible we lacked the necessary extraordinary imagination to align all the voices that came asking of us, lacked the creative powers to prioritize correctly, lacked the strength to tell the right stories at the right time, and lacked finally the ability to tell the future. I thought – and in fact I still think – that our imagination *was* adequate or that no one's was, that what was required was something superhuman. In any case, like I'd said before – we became corrupted. At first it appeared to us that we were doing the right thing, that we were just being cunning and sly with our resources and opportunities. But gradually what we thought was right became wrong. It became confusing. The stories we told to ourselves and others at first seemed no different to those we'd always been telling. The difference was so slight we didn't even know when what we were saying had turned into lies.

"One evening an FBI agent contacted me. At first he pretended he was a businessman and spoke at length about contracts and securing rights, distribution and payback. But something didn't make sense in his story. My instincts kicked in. He sensed he was losing me. On the other hand, we were flirting. We were attracted to each other despite our roles. It wasn't an irresistible attraction but it was strong and began to cloud my head. I'm not sure if the same was true for him or if he saw it only as another advantage for him to use.

"He made a gamble and confessed he was an agent. He said Papá was under investigation and it was only a matter of time. He said I could help and in return I would be granted amnesty. I didn't think they had any evidence, only innuendo, only a triangulation of circumstance—but I knew also that it would be painful to be accused, that no good would come of it.

"I was in a bind. On the one hand I felt no small attachment to the power I indirectly wielded through Papá. On the other hand, and of this I'm sure, Papá would have sold me out without a second's hesitation if he thought he could come out on top.

"I played the game very carefully from then on. Eventually I came to understand they needed more particular proof, something solid. It was I who proposed that the agent and I get married. 'He'll only trust family,' I said.

"We were married quickly, shortly thereafter, in a simple civil ceremony. The night we were married we made love for the first time. We got along very well. I hadn't expected it, how well we got along, so my judgment again became clouded. It took strength and a constant reminder that my primary goal was self-preservation.

"One night Papá found my husband in his office rooting around his papers. My husband was caught completely red-handed because he too, I think, had had his judgment clouded. Otherwise why would he rush and risk his outcome like that when patience was obviously the best course of action? My husband made some excuse and Papá let him leave his study and pretended he hadn't noticed anything.

"Papá was shockingly efficient. Two weeks later my husband was dead. The autopsy said it was an undiagnosed heart condition, but to me it was as clear as day that the man who looked like my father had poisoned my husband who was an undercover agent. From then on Papá was more circumspect with me, even more careful—and also any incriminating evidence was absolutely destroyed. He—and therefore I—had won. We'd achieved our goal of preservation and furthermore for a short but important time afterward we even flourished.

"But I entered a confused era in my life from which I only eventually and only partially ever escaped. It's true I wanted the man who resembled my father to win, to not get caught, to crush his enemies and thereby demonstrate and make manifest his indomitable powers. But I also wanted this other man, my husband—this *boychick*—to also succeed, to have the purity of his convictions rewarded, to find his glistening subterranean idealism reflected in the world of mundane transactions. I loved his beauty and his innocence and his sense of his own fate. If it had turned out the other way no doubt I would have been destroyed. So for my own sake and even from my most privately held point of view the right man had won. But I was disappointed that this had to be the case."

Mu'nisah stopped and pointed to the pneumatic tube set into the wall. I looked at my watch. She was right. We were due for our appointment with the captain.

I scribbled a note to YJ to come fetch us.

EVERYTHING BECAME simple when we entered the captain's quarters. It was clear what our roles were even as what we did was also entirely obscure to ourselves.

As we entered, a ten-piece brass band was exploding over and over again. A brassy, repeating nuclear detonation with a swing beat. The room darkened as we entered and a spotlight was aimed at the drummer.

Mu'nisah yelled into my ear that the drummer was the captain.

I looked more closely. The captain was in Bermuda shorts and had on pink tennis shoes. She had wild, long gray hair and a T-shirt with an image of a tuxedo on it. I'd guess she was in her sixties, but it was hard to get a bead because she kept vibrating like she was having a seizure and the ten-piece kept making its mind-scrambling brassy detonations.

YJ gestured to some seats. As Mu'nisah and I sat down the music shifted. The horns muted their explosions into philosophical wha-whas and then they faded out altogether and the captain took over with a quiet then loud then very loud drum solo, which frankly speaking was more berserk conniption than musical firework. Mu'nisah and I listened and sipped from another round of Rittenhouse Manhattans that YJ had kindly brought us.

The captain started scatting then. Or, to be more accurate, she began making brief yawps between idiot drum spasms.

"Fip mek dolly wolly!"

Drdrdrdr — clash — shwompin — crsh — crsh — drdrrdr.

"Migraine kroop-TAH!"

Ch-kchahkchah — whoomp — whoomp — crsh — crsh — krshh — ksch — ksh — ksh.

"Gadfly Nelly HOOF-ah!"

Badah-dah-dah-da-da-da—hdah—ddah—dddrdr—dah—krsh!

Then the ten-piece came back and settled into a very tarty yet very amateur version of "'Round About Midnight."

This didn't go on for very long (and in fact the whole thing happened so fast I could barely grasp it) and the next thing I noticed was that the captain was standing up. She'd gotten up and someone had slid behind her and taken over the kit literally without missing a beat. The spotlight followed the captain as she made her way downstage toward a microphone. She cradled it in her hand and began to sing in an unstable melody:

> Row row row your boat
> Gently down the dream
> Strangely strangely strangely
> Life is but a stream…

The band stopped suddenly and then the lights went out. Evidently the show was over. YJ came by with a flashlight to lead us out of the pitch-dark room. As Mu'nisah and I were being led out, the captain took the opportunity to purr a judgment into the microphone. Her amplified stage whisper surrounded us, filling up the dark. She said, "I pronounce you! I pronounce you! I pronounce you!"

YJ CLOSED THE DOOR behind us and we found ourselves outside the captain's quarters where all was silent again. The air smelled good and I felt suddenly exhausted. YJ asked Mu'nisah if she knew the way off the ship. She nodded. We shook hands then with YJ and said good-bye to him. I felt oddly very attached and was sad to see him go.

Before leaving the ship, Mu'nisah said she wanted to show me one more thing, a nice view off one of the ship's decks. She took my arm and led me back through the bowels of the ship and then up flights to finally a deck that looked out onto the dark waters, now reflecting city lights and car lights from bridges. We looked out for not too long and then, as it was wonderfully apparent we were going to kiss, we held off excitedly for a few minutes more. I was suddenly aware of how good a time I'd been having, which, during that period of my life, was rare. I was surprised to be enjoying myself. A moment later, after we had indeed kissed— and in truth kissed for a deliciously long time—I described to Mu'nisah my feelings of surprise. She only smiled and shrugged coyly and then took me by the hand and led me off the ship and back to her motorcycle.

# II. DOUBLE EXPOSURE

# Y J

A T FIRST NO ONE thought Henry was an idiot. That's important. That came later when I stopped knowing who he was. Even though I was with him almost every day until the end, I had stopped knowing who he was. But at first no one thought he was an idiot. In fact, everyone thought that he was rather smart. Because no one knew him. He would show off even. His showing off was not special but normal and because he really wasn't sure of it yet and thought it might be important to appear smart. It probably is. I still show off in non-show-offy ways, which is why I think I'm a good DP. He appreciated that.

Henry and I had both been born abroad and that most likely cemented our relationship. There were racial conflicts within him no doubt but you could hardly tell and he could hardly tell. These were deeply set contradictions for which he achieved solutions early on. I had dealt with my own set of contradictions by, from an early age, never having left New York City and I'm really not Chinese-American but, to be more accurate, Chinese-Manhattan. Not really contradictions but I guess they are unconscious forced choices or conscious choices forever held in stasis. By the time I met him that stuff was all comfortable jokes that rarely got anyone riled up but we both knew what skin we were. My name is Yuang Jing but everyone calls me Why Jay.

I was his cinematographer. He gave me minimal direction but got what he wanted. Or, he seemed satisfied with what I gave him. We made several pictures together and a thousand side projects, experiments. I'd met him at the movie theaters.

After a term of aggressive, obsessive attendance at the circuit of arthouses, museum theaters, and microcinemas, some stood out from the retirees and blue moon hooky players. These were the recognizably hardcore set who willingly and regularly traded their daylives for fakenight. At first we were reluctant to approach each other because solitude was part of the good taste. But eventually we knew each other, broaching ground in dusty review-lined foyers, encounters perfumed with liquid butter and glass cleaner. Iris-adjusting, stepping through doors into the shadows of day-embarrassed shabby marquees, we made acquaintance as vampires might, by our shared addiction.

How it began was one day a friend of ours committed suicide and we were devastated so we decided to make a movie. It didn't happen like that — there were many months between the suicide and the announcement of our intention — but that's the way I see it. Maybe that's the lie of history or maybe that's really how it happened. Philosophers are the silliest sort of people. Making the movie might have been my idea. If it was I'm very proud.

This first movie was nothing but it led to something. I'm not sure if that's true. Maybe when the something came, it came of itself and was not dependent on the nothing before. That seems unlikely. I take back what I said about philosophers, but only on occasion. I shot the first movie on a cheap consumer cam. It was beautifully pixelated in an unbeautiful way but whose beauty becomes manifest by context. Is it just me or does speaking truthfully require abstracting everything to vagueness. To vagary? To vagaries? To vaguenesses. Even then. It's a problem I'm not going to get caught up in right now.

The first movie was ten minutes long and on which we spent months. The plot was that two friends go driving at late dusk. Though I said it was nothing, I still like it. Henry and I are the friends in the car. I said I shot it but when I was in it, he shot it, but I lit it. Our friend who died's funeral was where we were driving from. Not really where we're driving from but fictionally. Henry said that what motivated it could be sentimental if we didn't show it.

In the film the sun is sunk and magic hour-y and in the course of the movie the darkness comes to surround us. It's a country road and the dash's light is a mix of pastelish colors I pushed, mostly the turquoise. This plays off our faces in a way that is unbelievable but pretty and makes me look a little sickish but him for some reason angelic. I'm talking a mile a minute, a whole monologue that Henry wrote that sounds adlibbed but was mostly written. About my (our friend's) dreams and fears, a thing about eco-terrorism that was just a kick Henry was on, and how beautiful the field next to us was. Throughout also, I tell an unending series of lousy jokes that are very nerdy and not even really jokes but random factoids from which jokes could have been fashioned but weren't. After we finished shooting, after Henry thought we had enough, he pulled the car over to the roadside and had a good cry. I sat next to him speechless. This would have been, according to Henry, when I mentioned it later, too dramatic to put in the movie. Later on I think he might have had a different view. That is, later, he tried to look at such things as best as he could, face on.

Editing it was where the movie came together. Henry was good at this from the beginning. He had had me shoot us at several different angles, inside and outside of the car, moving and not moving. And from this he made a flow of images that just interrupted the previous so that the whole appeared a constantly shifting, constantly falling acrobat's trick. The film just catching itself to fall again. It went with the monologue and the whole thing climaxed with a flood of bright white light and a truck's dopplering horn — moviespeak for close call. We submitted it to the festivals but nobody wanted it. People said the editing was too jumpy and that it was too long. Later on, of course, we got our revenge.

We kept working. When one of us got a little glum we'd say, "Let's go to the movies!"

(Though one understands what someone means when they refer to a song or songs as making up the soundtrack to their lives, a similar metaphor here would be deficient in describing our mania for, and relationship to, the movies we saw. It wasn't that they colored our mood but rather transformed our eyes and ears into cameras and microphones in order that we could continue the movies after their final frame. Our lives were the movies to our movies.)

(Which would have led to madness, its piling on of artificiality upon artificiality and its preference of the imaginary to the actual, its sight never unframed, its constantly deferred reality. Except that eventually it became unmistakable that we didn't have microphones for ears or cameras for eyes.)

"Let's go to the movies!"

After our matinees we inevitably went to the park and sat with takeout coffee. I bummed us a smoke and we reclined like two Adonis on a park bench, masters of the universe.

OTHER DAYS — less triumphant with puerile triumphs — we sat at home all day, television muted but screening a run-down copy of *Annie Hall* or *Tristana* or *Pink Flamingos* or *Dune*, playing tetris on a beatup laptop for quarter bets. We always had two screens going at once, the laptop where we played hours of tetris and the overly red-tinted pawnshop telly on which we used to watch our collection of salvaged VHS tapes. Usually we were silent, letting the muted images on the television's screen encode the air — even when our back was turned to it — with dialogue and music and sound long ago memorized by sheer repetition. A sound in mind — more rich than the tinny game music, the click

of our frantic keyboarding, our puffed curses — so that, at pivotal
moments in the films, we would look at each other to karaoke
from prompts of bounced light thinner by needs than gossamer:

> "A relationship, I think, is like a shark. You know? It
> has to constantly move forward or it dies. And I think
> what we got on our hands is a dead shark."

and then without laughing, without *acknowledging* what we were
doing was mimicry, was performance, was the ritual of religion
— we continued our game.

But other times we talked, and not surprisingly we spoke
about our mania, this encroaching thing. And once in a while it
would get pragmatic and I or he would say:

"Let's make a movie."

And *one* day I or he said:

"Let's make a movie."

And he or I said:

"What of?"

"Oh I don't care. How about —"

"— a war film."

"A war film?"

"A war film."

"A war film!"

❖ ❖ ❖

I was his cameraman and Noona was his lead, but Henry, after
weeks of shooting, kept us both in the dark up until the very last
moment. Neither one of us had seen the final cut when Henry

organized its premier. This first showing was the smallest and in many ways the best. I mean it was very pure. Mostly just cast and crew and friends. In the rented basement of a neighborhood social club, we gathered unprepared and happily, in a cool spring night. We involved ourselves in our senseless and habitual patterns of smalltalk: viciously gossiping, railing against the president and against the environment's end-days and the pimps in charge of the art business, one-upping each other's messianic anecdotes, comparing rents.

A half dozen shorts preceded *Imetay ofway ethay Olfway*, culled from various constellations in our little galaxy. We watched our offspring, marveling at their tottering, at their above-average marks, sighing at their poor showing on the ball field. Those movies were just like us! And in between, as Barry set up the projector for each, we sipped from warm beer bottles or paper cups of tea or glass flasks of cheap bourbon.

I remember being excited and nervous. It was a wonderful shock to see *Imetay ofway ethay Olfway* thread through the projector and open up the room in light. Gradually it would silent even the quiet murmuring, take us up in its weird magic. A secular rapture, a continuum of frozen dusk peopled by happy Sisyphuses, scorched with ever-mourning yet also deathless, the dead's dreams, dreams of the dead.

I walked immediately out when it was over. Made sure to catch Henry's eye and give him a smiling wink, to let him know how I felt. My leavetaking after that would say the rest. He'd understand. I was very much overwhelmed.

SOON AFTER, we did several more small screenings, wherever we could find a space — galleries, record shops, public gardens, basketball courts. Our big break was when G. Bianco, the film critic for *The Gotham Crier,* unexpectedly showed up to one of our screenings. Henry had sent him a letter, but no one thought he'd actually show up. Projected on the wall of a friend of a friend's father's haberdashery, two dozen or so colleagues and sympathizers sat on folding chairs when the critic wordlessly entered. We knew who he was, all having studied his author photo privately. The "G" stood for Gilbert. The room went silent.

In that creepy and utter quiet Barry threaded the projector as usual, and for ninety minutes — we held our breath. Everyone anxiously and regularly stole glances the critic's way.

After the credits Bianco left, as he'd arrived, without uttering a word. But as soon as the door closed the room broke into a buzz. Speculation was voluble and intense on the nothing that he had given as a hint to his opinion. Then we dispersed, like any other night ... I'd actually forgotten about it when the following Wednesday I casually picked up *The Crier.* As was my habit, I read the political cartoons, scanned my horoscope, and turned finally to Bianco's column. Where, jawdropped, I read the following:

> Watcher, take note: a local cine-troupe is peddling their wares, washing across Brooklyn's shore a brand-new vagueness, putting up ragtag screenings in venues as humble as social clubs, school gymnasiums, and hat shops. The collective calls itself The Flying Horses — and their debut film is a stunner.

Evidently shot in the past season on no budget (this not, as per usual, pardon), *Imetay ofway ethay Olfway* is an apocalypse-always autumnscape, a real-honest-to-god extravaganza, directed by Henry Yoo and starring local talent, Noona Göoterowski.

Part disaster film, part Keystone Cops, part nature walk, *Imetay ofway ethay Olfway's* motley crew traipses through the woods after an unspecified catastrophe. Their trip—and the movie—is conducted via a series of razzle-dazzle set pieces: dream sequences, ragged vaudeville, theatrical back-and-forths worthy of a Bergman chamber piece, and one non-distracting animated sequence. The hodgepodge, lovingly held together by a cinema personality as integrous and probably as ineffable as Efron Blum, undulates between bathos and gallows humor via an impressive choreography of actors' tics and camera angles. Luminous...

We read Gil Bianco's column religiously, each week, for both his bitchy zingers and his spot-on reviews. It was through him that we'd first learned the names of our pantheon, and it was especially through Gil that we'd followed the career of the filmmaker we most admired, Efron Blum. To have a glowing review from Bianco was a feather in our cap. To be name-checked with Blum was glory.

Bianco's review opened the door to the major festivals and six months later a small company, Ugly Avatar Studios, picked up *Imetay* for distribution—not coincidentally this was also Blum's distributor.

This mid-sized fame we achieved that year was a druggy type of satisfaction. It had a similar thrill, a likewise attendant depression, and, more than pleasure, was characterized by its many long-lingering consequences.

P ROBABLY THE most significant was Henry's friendship with Efron Blum. This was made possible again by Gilbert Bianco, who liked above all to matchmake, to champion, to gossip — a type without which nothing would ever get done.

Gil held a dinner party one night in his tastefully appointed Midtown apartment. His longtime partner, Paul Hicks, was there. So were Efron Blum and his wife Sveta. They all looked older and elegant and when Henry and I arrived, I had the distinct feeling of being unimportant. Noona, who gave the group its courage, was sick that night. She was bitter about missing it, but I think I was more bitter about being abandoned by her. I sorely missed her strength, especially when attempting, over dinner, to make conversation with Efron and Gil. I tried two or three openings, but each time Gil would wince vividly and Efron would merely nod. Finally, as if to say enough is enough, Gil gave me a thin-lipped smile that clearly told me not to speak to him again.

I knew to follow orders and turned to Sveta to ask if I might make myself another Tom Collins. The rest of my evening was taken up with Sveta, Paul and myself exchanging vacation tales.

Meanwhile Henry was having a much more momentous evening. I would periodically cast envious glances across the room where Efron, Gil, and Henry had retired after dinner. What in a personality makes one a servant? What in *mine* I wondered, and have kept wondering, but nonetheless have no answer but fact.

E FRON BLUM from that evening on became a great mentor to Henry. Not so much an influence as far as Henry's art went but a considerable one in that leftover arena, his life. For a short while he even aped Efron's Brooklynese, his dandyish wardrobe, his taste for sweet wines.

Efron was independently wealthy. Henry was too, incidentally —phenomenally so it turned out—but he actively kept it hidden. While Efron never specifically disclosed that he "had money," everyone knew he didn't work and that he nonetheless lived in high style with his Bosnian wife, Sveta. They maintained a handsome apartment in the West Village and another in Key West. His reputation was based initially on a series of short films he had made as a young man. They had various concrete subjects—commuters, trees, restaurant diners, trains, deserts—which he captured with a specially modified animator's camera and which, through a muscular and virtuosic editing, he abstracted into poetry. After this celebrated work he had had a great difficulty finding his way. He told Henry later about this period, that he didn't want to repeat himself, but—felt completely out of ideas. He gradually sunk not entirely out of sight but into a limbo of mediocre work. His middle age saw a series of lackluster films and miserable marriages.

Everyone had considered him washed up, or, at best a film genius who had done his finest work as a young man. Then, strangely, in his mid sixties when people barely remembered his name, Blum began producing odd pieces of video. Mysterious, self-erasing or self-denying narratives, these videos were often infused with a frantic editing style that eclipsed even his own earlier manic cutting and were made primarily possible by the then brand-new technologies of digital editing. Critics (led by Bianco) announced Blum's late style as majestic and masterful. They spun a biography of the artist who had survived inferno and infamy, who had in fact been tempered by them, and who now returned with, so to speak, news for the people. So, anyway, went the story, and for the first time in a long while Blum enjoyed some success.

It was around this time that we met him. As they shared a certain temperament and as both Henry's and Efron's respective stars were then on the rise, they found immediately that they had a great deal to talk about.

I know Henry asked Efron's advice on our upcoming shoot. It was a complicated one, our group's second feature. We were anxious to see if we could succeed again. As well, Henry insisted we up the ante in terms of both our thematic and technical ambitions. We called it *Oodgay Eye-bay, Agondray Innway.*

The basic plot is as follows:

Ghost haunts, theater creaks, voyeurs watch. Wind blows, cloud obscures, fog hides, rain pours. Then murderer kills, criminal plots, robber steals, adulterer betrays, vampires suck, agent spooks. To relieve, sexkitten vamps and comedian punchlines. But this doesn't finally distract from communists meeting, artists brooding, governments ruling, ill faltering. In time though, superhero flies, toughguy kicks, detective solves, and nurse aids. To give some context and 'humanize' it, sleeper sleeps, sleeper wakes, woken rises, and risen breakfasts. Later, diner lunches, worker works, watcher boobtubes, fatigued sups, and lastly, sleeper sleeps. It was hard to figure out how to do it, technically, but eventually we also film: thinker thinks. Also, with carefully chosen film stock to accentuate the action, walker steps, runner sprints, catcher snags, jumper leeeeeaps! Hurler, for the record, hurls. But before the final credits, ghost haunts, criminal escapes, and murderer smiles.

B Y THE TIME we finished *Oodgay Eye-bay, Agondray Innway* Henry and Efron had emerged from a period of infatuation with each other and had settled into one of utter reliance. This reliance would manifest itself in night-long, even week-long, conversations, and really this entire period could be described as one long, uninterrupted dialogue between the elder and the younger filmmaker. And the purpose of this conversation I would say was one where the two would, artfully and with various and strategic extended metaphors, praise the other.

From the outside — as indeed I was — it seemed vapid and indulgent. I would try to discuss it with Noona. (I thought of Noona and myself as, at the time, united, as if we were both wives of cheating husbands.) But Noona's participation in these sessions was one, in hindsight, of a controlled sympathy. But I was blind to her restraint and would complain — always barely

hidden in acrid, humorless jokes — of the language Efron and
Henry seemed to be inventing, an exclusive one, made entirely
for the purpose of fawning over one another.

Noona would remind me that they depended on one another
not merely for flattery but specifically for the other's criticisms,
which more often than not echoed their own and by the concur-
rence gave them the strength to clearly face their own deficien-
cies. But I only continued to complain about my friend and told
Noona that such a dependency between two artists could not last.

That my opinion was prescient turned out to be hollow victory.

F OR OUR THIRD film Henry asked Efron to act, to play, in
fact, himself. A self-reflexive story, the plan was to make a
movie about movie making. Titled *Irmaway Epvay,* the film is
also the story of a couple's breakup.

The basic plot is as follows:

Anna is a beautiful housewife married to John, a scriptwriter
with ambitions in the theater. John has been hired by George, a
producer, to help rewrite a contested film-adaptation of Homer's
*Odyssey.* George soon reveals that he has designs on Anna. The
film begins on a studio lot, and in fact the movie's first shot is of
myself setting up for a long tracking shot. The movie is in large
part a very self conscious recreation of the dilemma of making
films for the market place. It features not only a cartoon version
of the investor-producer as idiot dictator but also a lionized
version of the film director as artist-hero. This latter role Henry
asked Efron to fill, which he happily agreed to do. Alongside this

critique of film economics a considerable part of the movie is made up of a long sequence shot in Anna and John's apartment. There, they argue about various things: about their future, about their mortgage, over John's participation in George's film, about their sleeping arrangements. Eventually, in the film's end, Anna leaves John. She drives away with George in his red Alfa-Romeo. However, soon after, in an absurd highway accident, George and Anna are killed. The film's last scene is of John watching Efron (whose character is named "Efron Blum") directing a scene for the now (perhaps only temporarily) producer-less film.

A film about a film, *Irmaway Epvay,* along with further positive reviews, led by Bianco's example, increased our audience by a factor but did not—as both Henry and Efron had predicted—catapult us from "cult" status. In terms of ticket sales, *Irmaway Epvay* was our most successful picture, a disappointing high-water mark for all of us.

NOONA WAS beautiful. But not uncommonly so. You see her type of beauty every two city blocks. A cute bob, athletic legs, an intelligent face with a sly, warm smile. But what is captivating about her is the same thing that makes her a great actress. That is, she is a master of the intimate situation. Or, to be more precise, she is a master of that situation where a few people are in a room. With objects or numbers or books, she's not much better or worse than you or me. But in a room with another person—or up to a dozen other persons—she is in control, and in fact can achieve almost any effect.

Noona's materials, so to speak, are the energies of the people around her, are the surrounding personalities. They need not be of a particular type, and I've seen her deliver crackling performances surrounded by the dullest or simplest type of actors. If you watch her films you'll see her weakest scenes are those when she is all alone. At these times she seems relatively mechanical. Of course even in these scenes there is the camera and behind that—the rest of us. I have always wondered what Noona is like completely alone, a sublime impossibility.

Perhaps her blankness, her pliability comes from her deep past—one she barely remembers. A foreigner, she was orphaned when her home nation was divided by war. Or perhaps my idea is ridiculous, and it's a fool's errand to try and pinpoint the sources, modes and limits of an artist. My definition in any case was created over a long period of time and in addition was one crafted from close scrutiny.

I was present at Noona and Efron's first meeting. Efron and Sveta were having Henry, Noona, and myself over for dinner. Noona was—as we'd all been—a long-time admirer of Blum's work. She could speak particularly knowledgeably on it and included that night comments on some of his lesser-known middle pieces—a fact which flattered and impressed Blum I'm sure. This was definitely not Noona's most subtle performance, but because of my understanding of her talents, it is my opinion that all that came after was somehow her provocation.

The entire night was sprinkled with her questions such as "Mr. Blum, in your film X, how did you…?" or "Efron, what did you do to get...?" or "But Efron, did you realize what you were doing when...?" Furthermore all of us were falling into place, that night, falling into character. In the scene, Noona and Efron had the leads: the studious actress meets the accomplished older director. If it had been a film script we would have laughed at its transparency, at its formula. As this however was life we each felt a strange magnetic pull into our respective cardboard roles, as if the dramatic formulas that we disparaged so much in movies were seeking a final revenge by becoming inevitable in our own lives.

Noona began an affair with Efron.

A T FIRST, they both acted with extreme discretion. Noona was "with" Henry, Efron was married to Sveta, and above all Henry was a best friend to them both. Around this time too, Efron—without, I believe, the slightest feeling of hypocrisy or malice—hired Henry to be the assistant director on his next film.

Noona surprised me by making me the confidante of her affair. I was surprised not only because Henry was my boss, he too was *my* best friend, and in fact—the love of my life. I thought of this latter fact as an open secret, something which I thought we all realized but to save face and to continue to deny the painful impossibility of this love, I thought everyone had simply decided, privately and individually, to keep silent about it. Perhaps the "open" secret was less so than I'd thought, but even now I find that hard to believe.

Nonetheless to my shock a few weeks after the affair had begun Noona told me about it. (Henry in fact was, at the moment of Noona's confession to me, having dinner with Efron.)

Efron had simply called one day and said that they should meet and that she shouldn't tell Henry about it. "I thought maybe it was for a role," she said, laughing uncomfortably.

"No, not for a role," Efron had said when they met. And continued matter of factly, "I want to sleep with you. I want us to have dinners together. Take trips. And see movies together. And I want to do this all in secret from Henry and from my wife."

"I think he's done it before," Noona said to me.

DURING NOONA's confession and afterwards, to her, I was a consummate friend, begging the right details, pardoning and commending just enough of her guilty excitement over the affair. But inside, and to myself, I truly felt like giggling. Henry cuckolded!

It was as simple as having the tables finally turned. And furthermore, in a fevered delusion, as a kind of final grasp, I anticipated some kind of breakup. An opening of some kind. Perhaps a return to a former intimacy between Henry and myself. Maybe even...

THIS OF COURSE was insane, but I was. And so, within this little drama, I'd figured out at last my own role: Iago.

I waited for the absolute worst moment for Henry and Efron, right in the heat of production for Efron's film. During a time

I knew when things were going poorly, one night, when Henry I knew would be exhausted from the day's shoot, I asked him over for dinner. And I colored my invitation with just the lightest urgency.

Henry, my friend, has always exhibited only compassion for me, especially during my life's various crises, and he caught the note right away, and—agreed to come over.

"I don't know how to tell you this," I said. It's so peculiar how such sentences appear, pre-fabricated in the mind, perfect for the given occasion. And in fact it isn't only sentences that appear this way but entire emotions. Not only are we constantly under the tyranny of received ideas but, it seems to me, many entire lives are simply the enactment of predesigned—and not thoughtfully either!—blueprints. I said, "Efron and Noona are having an affair."

Henry did not move for a moment. He did not become en-raged. "Tell me," he said.

I told him what I knew, all that Noona had told me, and that I'd kept it a secret from him. I asked his forgiveness but pleaded, cunningly I thought, that I had been torn between two loyalties.

He then immediately left my apartment. It's funny, now, to think at that moment I did not fear for Henry's life.

Before Henry killed himself I remember often having the fear that he would—though there were no unsuccessful attempts, not even talk save that self-euthanasia was always a theme in his work. But this deception of mine took place in the period just prior to that sadder one, and when Henry left my apartment I was almost rubbing my hands together in glee, like a cartoon villain, in anticipation of the drama I had just set in motion.

Bᴜᴛ I was to be disappointed, mostly.
It's true that Henry immediately confronted Efron, who admitted everything, and that Henry quit his production and that the two never spoke again. But the rupture I was really looking forward to, and which was the true goal of my engineering—the one between Noona and Henry—never took place.

To my chagrin the two huddled together even more fiercely, like travelers in a storm. They at first barricaded themselves in their apartment, an impenetrable fortress, which for a week yielded to neither phone call nor visit. Then, the two went off on an impromptu trip to Europe for two months.

I spent that remaining hot summer alone, simmering and disappointed and bereft. And when they did return, when Henry and Noona again appeared, a couple, I was in an instant again there at their side—but only as before, a sidekick, a member of the audience. You will imagine my disappointment, even though bitterly anticipated during those hot months, at discovering myself again and still, on the outside.

# NOONA

W E LEAVE New York after an episode of heartbreak, of infidelity. It is an early stage to our relationship, and I must have been unconsciously testing it, seeing if it could break. Henry and I had fallen together maybe too easily, I thought, had fallen into a default love based on superficial commonalities (we were both orphaned twins, foreign-born, estranged from our families). And so the infidelity was part of the courtship, in fact a part where Henry had to—in which I demanded that—Henry compete and conquer and win. Something brutally simple like that. Efron was a sad, powerful, dying king. Who was commanding and elegant while ordering waiters at restaurants. And who sat evenings listening to symphonies, alone on his couch, obliterating his mind with Scotch. Who made a handful of beautiful films—films which resonated with a pitch unfelt before or since. Who made love like a bear attacking, lumbering and violent and with unexpected grace. Who, with fingers stained and smelling of tobacco, would circle my clit, caress me, while in a quiet guttural voice thrill himself by whispering threats of violence.

After Europe, I never see Efron again. The trip—along with the indiscretion and its make-up—couple Henry and I more than ceremony. But to make sure we bully a wedding out of a befuddled country priest in Provence. So, when we come back from Europe, we're married.

Now, I've a child-groom who's also a wunderkind and a semi-glittery life—costume jewelry on an armpit-haired queen, the type—that I'm thankful for. Also, YJ—his lapdog loyalties, the calming presence of his constant scheming, its undertones, the necessary distraction of him. And the troupe and the calendar of productions that we fill to brimming. So as to never die.

Armed thusly the time passes so momentously and so quickly that I'm breathless. Fallouts are only transitions between events. The cycle a perennial motion of whitewater. Some days I'm unspeakably sad. Just for, I'd hazard to guess, the rush of happinesses—each too fast to pass to digest. And the dismal future guaranteed by peaks.

The Flying Horses obeys its self-powered green light to the max of its power and we begin what will turn into three years of almost straight production. The next is an autobiographical tale that Henry, YJ and I spin out over a week of dinners. We think we'll shoot it quickly, most of it through guided improvisation. It will be a movie about a relationship that falls apart over an infidelity—an old story and also an autobiographical one. Henry and my situation differs from the movie in that we stay together and the couple in the film falls apart, but—the fight scenes are more or less documentary. We name it *Arispay, Exastay.*

The plot is as follows:

Boy meets girl meets boy meets boy meets boy meets girl meets boy meets girl meets girl meets boy meets boy meets boy meets boy meets boy meets girl meets girl meets boy meets boy meets boy meets boy meets girl meets boy meets girl meets boy meets girl meets girl meets girl meets boy meets girl meets girl meets boy meets girl meets boy meets girl meets boy meets girl meets boy.

W E SHOW it at what Henry and YJ insist is a film festival but really has turned into our semi-private yearly party. Of making films—the bored waiting, the moment of acting, the release from that moment—I remember mostly only when I see the movie in a theater, maybe the first time with an audience. These filmfests then are particularly momentous for me. At that time, then peculiarly does the scaffolding appear, so I remember the moments before "Action!" is called and after "Cut!" All of a sudden the mechanics of the production are conjured in my mind just as, for everyone else, a seemingly effortless appearance manifests. One sweats under hot lamps, but—it's never seen! What would it mean, I wonder, to not hide it...

The audience, our chosen audience, loves it. These fests are in a way guaranteed, a preaching to the choir, which Henry needs to satisfy some boyish longing. And we tolerate it because *we* love it! How much fun it is! To be a star and to be constantly engaged and thought engaging. There's a slight pressure but the event's energy feeds you for a night.

Whereas the time between such showings — reality, so to speak — is not like this, is perfectly inessential. In the end we prefer reality; we realize that inessentiality is, in fact, truer. But gluttony is momentarily tempting and especially tempting in memory. Nonetheless we are not so stupid; we are fortunate to not (yet) be so stupid.

The time after this production turns into a rare stretch, about three months, where we are not promoting anything, not negotiating anything, not studying anything, not in any sort of step of production. We are merely ourselves. At first, without anything to distract us, Henry and I almost break up.

The first month we fight constantly.

First about Efron.

And then because he wants to decorate the apartment radically and I want it to be comfortable. And then another night, about Efron. And then because we have to have too many dinners with people we don't enjoy, or with people only one of us enjoys. And then because we never go out. And then about Efron. And then because he or I am a petty bourgeois whore who deserves to have his or my head on a stick.

And then we settle down. Change is hard but in this case swift. We luck into a great apartment in Fort Greene and after our domestic battles — squabbles really — over interior design, we adorn with a compromised but tasteful austerity. Now it is us who sit, together, scattered around a sizeable sunken living room like two lonely teeth in a beggar's mouth, guiltily reading fashion magazines and catching up on the Greek tragedies we missed since we were truants and refugees and orphans. We happily burrow into our affluence, engulfed each of these nights with a thankful warmth, of a content feeling of inclusion within a long unbroken line of comfortable humanity. I would think of myself as having grown complacent if I was not so grateful for it all. Looking over at Henry I know he feels the same, who taps his foot gently to the music on the radio, a mild and mournful air. We appear dead but are in fact at peace.

SUCH PEACE does not last however and a few months later we embark on our next fart in the age of mechanical repo-men. Our next film is one which finds us in a meditative mood. YJ says that the film's content—mysterious, internal, abstract—is so because our placid exteriors, our current life-calmness, is hiding a rising existential dilemma, of which the movie is merely a mild expression and also only a bookmark before an explosive and tragic denouement. "Still waters run deep," he says.

Called *Irrormay,* it is shot in black and white video alternating with lurid drenched colors.

The plot is as follows:

To me, it's our finest achievement. Honest and moving and with it, too, I think we've finally mastered or articulated our group's particular inkblot of paranoia, aggression, wit and energy.

Of course nobody sees it.

Except for those who do — who hate it.

Gilbert Bianco does his best to like it, but his effort shows. The distributors are polite in their rejection. Indifference is the majority opinion; pity and antipathy the two minority ones.

*Irrormay* kerploops directly into the lake of time and we are astonished to watch it sink and turn instantly into void. What we fought for, and what we'd fought for so much more *consciously* than the previous films, and indeed what we'd thought was finally *something* — isn't. Is, we discover, less than shadow and ash.

YJ and I put our heads down, we rest them on the kitchen table for, let's be honest, months. We are aswirl in thick syrupy self-pity, which only clears for momentary durations, windows of either bitter protest or numbed routine, before resumes the cotton-candy-thick weather of gloom, the El Greco-eyed pathos, and the self-administered vodka.

Henry repeatedly tries to jostle us: "Assholes! Who do you think you are? Live a little."

But I'll have none of it. I lay in bed, a freak of disappointment. I've left out the work: how we slaved over, happily slaved over, *Irrormay*. We killed ourselves. We had hoped. And sweated blood. I keep the curtains drawn.

YJ is no better a sport. He gets into a habit of scrambling a nice chorizo omelet for an afternoon breakfast and washing it down with a pint of bourbon.

For months, that's the cartoon, but—no one's really laughing. And Henry can't sit still for that long. He gives up. He starts to ignore us and then goes off to work, he says, on a script. He takes off for New Mexico then Kansas then Indiana, staying in cheap motels with only a laptop and good American sunlight. Our savings dwindle, an hourglass we ignore.

YJ starts coming over to our place because he's lonely. He convinces me to drink. It seems to work for us. Laughing in fits at four in the afternoon because we're high and the cat farted and the fridge door is still open and because we're high. The goddamn TV and magazine idiot children of America, we say.

"Those pigs," YJ says.

"Who do you mean?" I say.

"You know," YJ says.

"You mean the goddamn TV and magazine idiot children of America?" I say.

"That's them," YJ says.

After a while we wonder where Henry's off to and call him to find he's in a Holiday Inn in Bainville, Montana—and he's working on a script. "Good, good," we say. And: "When can we see it?"

"Eh, stay drunk!" Henry says, "You're both good for nothing!" and hangs up the phone.

But the truth is, at that moment, we all love each other so we say goodbye to Henry unworried at the dead line, and YJ and I order in from Double Happiness or Wok and Roll with a growing confidence that everything might be turning for the better. But just in case, we decide to get drunk.

A month later, when Henry returns, we jump on him. "Where is it?"

"What?"

"Don't give us that! The script! The new script!"

"Oh," says Henry. "Well this time it's different. This time…" His voice trails before he finishes with: "I've an idea."

The following month we begin shooting on *Amingflay Eaturescray*.

FOR THIS shoot, Henry seems to be even more the visionary, wrapped up in a private spectacle-making. He purchases a cruise ship, accessing a hidden and terrifying wealth we never discuss, and announces it's the movie's only location. He stops talking, or will only speak a flow of inane silly jokes. He cries whenever he sees green so everyone is forbidden to wear it. He shouts and stamps, doing a too convincing imitation of an idiot. He dances and preens. He directs by feeble gesture, dedicated to uncommunicated principles, and we all hold our breath.

Yet in the end, *Amingflay Eaturescray* survives production with a rather beautiful and simple story intact.

Its plot is as follows:

EXHAUSTED FROM weeks of cycling boredom and blindfolded ecstasies, Henry abruptly announces the last day of the shoot. A joyless dumbfounded wrap occurs. We're wondering what indeed had happened — as we slink back to our meager lives less fortified with wonder than after any other Flying Horses shoot. Instead we return to our days, confused, subsisting on doubt, unhappily matured.

Then, a week later, we get word that Efron Blum has killed himself.

I am reasonably devastated but Henry seems to only absorb the seismic death wave so that little trace is visible, but — he is not unchanged. Though I yell at him it's the worst thing to not react, he nonetheless will only wear a stone face.

We torture each other for a short while and then let the grief sink into our loam, the volume of our communication doing a parallel tumble.

T HE NEXT MONTHS are gotten through. One day, eventually, feeling the right moment to press for an outcome, I suggest a vacation. We decide on something simple and drive to a coastal town to spend two weeks in a rented beachhouse.

Henry is differently silent during the trip, his silence changing from a shell into a medium. And I begin to take his silence, which extends into our lovemaking, as tender reflection of my own feelings. I begin to envelop myself in it—born in the beachhouse's must and of the surfsounds.

W HEN WE return we begin editing the footage together. Henry asks me if I'd like to edit with him. Continuing our lately established habit of silence, his question is asked almost wordlessly. Equally quiet I answer. So that this shift too, unprecedented yet natural feeling, is done smoothly, with no jarring transition. Our love, I can only think, is deepening.

Almost immediately, as we begin editing, we discover ourselves in a silent, writhing embrace. Each session starts furtive and we work far far from language, as the sex act is. In a cool black room, deep within and away from the world of our apartment, illuminated only by screen glow, we huddle dog-hunched and bent, quick-nodding and murmuring. Our hands move over the controls precisely, without negotiation or error besides play. It is an erotic event yet cold, mindless yet intelligent. Perhaps, we both think (we both hope) what is born from now will be also powerful, pure and savage.

And maybe he does, momently, think this way. And momently

we both do hope. But he cops out, finally, fades, lets his silence turn into mere quietude. Henry, in that critical moment, retreats. He stops coming into the office, stakes out permanent ground on the couch, sits sleeps and eats there. In other words, if editing the film had become a prolonged, teased, excited work of lovemaking—then Henry finishes prematurely.

Or loses interest. Or goes limp despite interest and not finishing. Leaving me revved, intent, near but unorgasmed.

I may love Henry intensely, perhaps even most, within that combination of non-tumescence and heat, but—I need to finish.

Whatever Henry had, what vision he expended or used, I pick up, or, create from it my own fantasy. What is born then is not born of sex, nor onanism, but of spastic spent vestigial mechanisms, of aimless aborted and exhausted acts, purposeless genitalia nonetheless rubbing. It was not fireless and in its opposition to goals, signed a limitless truth.

I finish the picture.

# III. SPOOKY ACTION AT A DISTANCE

He likes horror and sex movies, and James Bond.
— CHOI EUN-HEE

In fact, most people underestimate their capacity
to withstand pain.

— *CIA's Human Resource Exploitation Training Manual*, 1983

I T'S WHEN the cop is punching my face that I make the decision. I decide to go look for my sister. My whole life I'd indulged in a stupid thrill, a very risky habit. In the middle of the night I'd sneak through the town and deface posters of the beloved president. Sometimes just a mustache over his beloved pudgy face. I kept it scatological or primitive. For fifteen years I'd done this and never got caught.

The cop is working me over pretty good. I've never taken a punch before. I worry about my brain and whether he'll bust something inside me and I'll die slowly as things that aren't supposed to meet mix inside my sloshy guts. I'm a wet animal and I'm weeping like a child and very ashamed that I am and I'm scared.

He beats me up and then lets me go.

ONE OF the twins is me. They're playing a game of hide and-seek together, which—with only two people—is also tag, sardines in a can, capture the flag, and hot-and-cold. We didn't call our game any of those.

This is when we're eight. The war is looming but we don't know anything at all about that except an exhaustion familiar already in our bones and a subdermal panic that shimmies constantly up and down our backsides.

Even though I know now all kinds of impossible things about the bomb that is about to destroy our home, it always surprises me. For instance I know that the engineer who perfected its targeting system so that it can fly around corners was a Haitian educated in Canadian universities and now retired happily to Nantes, France. I know that the casing is coated with a polymer most commonly used today in plastic wrap and discovered accidentally by a Dow Chemical worker, that the nitroamine in the bomb was developed for the US government by the son of Jews escaped from the pogroms and that this explosive was, at the time, one of the most powerful in the world, used to begin fission reactions in nuclear weapons. The government that launched the bomb was an invading nation fighting another invading nation in our soon-to-be divided poor sap of a country in a ridiculous contest called a proxy war. Does it help to know your maker? I think they were aiming for a bridge a half mile south of us.

The girl I'm playing with is older than me by fourteen minutes. We share our father's analytic nature—he was a factory engineer —and our mother's depressive seasons. She's better than me at fighting, which embarrasses me since I'm a boy. I'm the better drawer and it's a tie when it comes to sums. Right now she's doing a slow count to ten with her eyes closed and her forehead pressed against a tree. I'm hidden behind a big rock that fell into the ditch that runs along the road to town and which we'd often use as a landmark to visitors. ("At the big pink rock in the ditch, turn left through the woods," we'd say.) When she gets to four, the bomb explodes our home and kills our parents.

How it usually works is you get beaten up, then they let you go for a couple of weeks—both so you can heal a little bit and so you can show up at work and everyone can see how you've had the shit beaten out of you. Then, a few weeks later, they send you off to the labor camps on trumped up charges and you are never heard from again.

I decide I'm going to make a run for it to go find my sister. It's something to be desperate. There are one or two people I can think of who just might have underground connections. But if I contact them I risk implicating them and what's more, it's likely that some of them are simply agents, lures.

There's a woman who I think might have it in her. I sneak over to her house at night and break in. I enter the bedroom and turn on the light. She sits up in bed and looks at me as if it's perfectly normal for a stranger to show up in her bedroom in the middle of the night. "Turn that off, you idiot," she hisses.

I start to explain but she only says, "Shut up. Did anyone see you come here? Anyone at all?"

"I don't think so," I say.

"You want to get out. Leave the country?"

"Yes."

"How much money do you have?" she asks.

THAT NIGHT I dream of the posters. I'm standing in front of a huge wall completely covered with propaganda posters. In my hand is a paint brush and at my feet is a small bucket of black paint. Unlike in real life, I take my time. I'm not rushed or sweating or excited. I'm only contemplating all the different possibilities.

Instead of defacing any individual poster, instead of giving the beloved president a Mohawk or tits or a tooth gap or devil's horns or blacking out his eyes—I ignore him. The huge wall becomes an enormous canvas and I feel free to paint however I please. I reach down and pick up the small bucket and dip the brush. The bristles suck in the dark paint. I lift the brush to the wall to make a mark. Sometimes it's a sweeping line, sometimes just a dot or a cramped squiggle. The dream keeps stuttering though and I never progress any further than that first mark. Even though I know that as soon as I continue, as soon as I elaborate on my subject the posters will start to fade and the wall will become pure canvas and my painting can manifest itself. My entire uncluttered being will, so to speak, appear. And yet— almost because I know how great this feeling could be—the dream won't progress. It stutters and repeats with infinite variations at its opening. I toss in the bed, tortured by the inability to make the dream move forward.

I wake up and wonder about the difference between being drunk and dreaming—both so-called illusory states.

I'm in a lot of pain still. I'm looking forward, it's strange but true, to either making it out or being caught and then shot. Either way, I feel it'll then be done.

T HERE IS really nothing to prepare, I realize, and somehow this thought above others depresses me. As rootless and as inconsequential—maybe even more so—as the day I was born. The four or five friends I get drunk with on the weekends I know will miss me, even as I know they're currently avoiding me. There's every reason in the world right now to not be seen with me—someone figuratively and actually marked for death. If our situations were reversed, I'd do the same to them. I only have myself to blame. For one reason or another I've always kept everyone at a distance.

I look around my small bachelor's apartment. A shelf full of useless books. A dozen lurid magazines, cheap pots and pans. Two radios that only receive the state station. The battered furniture that came with the rooms. Within these walls I have always done exactly as I'd pleased, which, it turned out, hasn't been much.

Without lifting a finger, I'm ready.

M Y SISTER's learned this from someone I don't know who. She wants to show me something. We go out at dusk when the cicadas are out. There are a lot of them. I turn to her and say,

So what did you want to show me? She says, Here, and pulls some string from her pocket. Then she crouches down. I crouch too. What are we gonna do? I ask. She flips a cicada onto its back. It whirs and tries to get up. My sister makes a small loop with the string and then ties a knot around the cicada's abdomen. Then she ties the other end of the string to her finger. Watch, she says. She stands up. The cicada continues to twitch and, as the string lifts the insect off the ground, it suddenly opens its wings and takes flight. But it is tethered by my sister's string. She holds her finger up and the cicada flies around her hand.

THE NEXT day at work is tough. I'm required to go and report myself to the boss. He acts furious. "You couldn't think about anyone else, huh? Now they're going to be all over this factory like flies on shit. That brings trouble for everyone you know. Now get the fuck out of my sight." He sounds angry but I know he's just sad and scared. He can't be seen or heard being nice to me. But while he's screaming at me, he slips me a foreign bill. It's a big gesture and there's nothing I can say.

I work at a publishing house, which in itself is a joke. We print the propaganda magazines and only a few different books: the biography of the great leader and the state-sanctioned history books and encyclopedia. Every home in the country already has a copy of each and every winter most of our print-run ends up being burned in fireplaces—though this of course is strictly illegal.

For the past ten years I was in charge of maintaining one of the large presses. I work with a group of six men and women.

That morning they are standing as a group when I approach. I nod and they nod back. A chair has been set in the corner for me. They obviously don't want me to work with them and I too don't think I can handle it. I just sit and stare at the ground.

The shelf next to me is crammed full of the beloved president's biography. Like everyone else, I know his story by heart. Other than my own body the thing I'm most familiar with is the beloved president. His spirit surrounds me constantly. My sister is a ghost I can barely recall, someone who keeps jumping out of the frame of my memories. I can't remember what she looks like. The face of the beloved leader on the other hand is always in front of me, laid over every scene, even, like an official seal, over those that contain his actual image, which I admit, are many. He is everywhere, inside and outside of me. I don't know where my sister is.

S ITTING IN the chair I transform. I become either a walking corpse or I'm a real man in a land of phantoms. I make a decision while staring at the floor. My coworkers, my boss, my friends — they've become figments. They're beyond death; they're colored air. I decide. I have to focus on my escape. If I survive, then much later I can remember them and mourn them and be ashamed. But I decide then. I'm going to make a full effort.

The two days at work are not without purpose. I sit in my wordlessly assigned chair from morning to dusk while colored air fails to distract me and the seemingly infinite repetition of the beloved president pulses next to me: the book's blue bindings forming a familiar and rhythmic call to submission, which I am not tempted by and anyway in which I've never believed. I strengthen my will.

(WHEN WE have to leave them, we tie our cicadas to a melon rind hoping they'd be alive the next day, which they never were.)

ON THE THIRD night, as we'd agreed, someone knocks on my window a little after two in the morning. I open it and whisper that the back door is unlocked. I hear that door open and close. I've been sitting in a chair in dim light, waiting.

She looks like a country peasant, sunburned and with coarse manners, but when she speaks she sounds like someone much better educated. I imagine she's a disgraced journalist or physics professor, banished to the fields. The first thing she says is the price. It's nearly all my money. I go to the bathroom, pull out the special purse I've made and hidden beneath my pants. I return to the main room and hand her the bills. She says to turn off the light and then she slips out the door again.

I sweat for thirty minutes in the dark, thinking I've been cheated. And then there's a knock on the glass. "What are you bringing?" she whispers through the open window. "Nothing," I say. She names an alley nearby. "Go there now," she says and disappears.

When I get there, I see a small truck with its engine idling. I go over to the passenger side and get in. In the shadows the driver looks like the husband or brother of the woman. He's got on a field-hand's outfit and gestures with the same rough, inarticulate manners, but after a few minutes I begin to suspect it's the same person, that the woman who took my money was actually this man in disguise. He starts driving and I stare ahead.

THE DRIVER tells me we're heading to a remote town several hours away. "From there someone else will take you. That's all I know."

I tell him, "This all seems better organized than I'd thought possible."

The driver allows himself a smile and says, "You're lucky. We've been admiring your artwork for some time. That's why people are making an effort even though you don't have much money."

I feel strange. I'd never spoken to anyone about my *artwork* and now, other than my policeman, and that by force, I still hadn't. Now my driver has referred to it openly.

"Yes, people are taking quite a chance. It's funny because, you must understand, you aren't even a very useful political person-ality — really just an over-aged vandal." But then, as if to make sure I have some strength left in me, he says softly, "Your defiance wasn't a small thing though, however conscious you were of it."

I realize he's asking me a question. I say, "Certainly I knew it could get me killed. Probably that's all. People like to see fools go where angels fear to tread — especially when they're caught and punished. Then they can happily pass judgment."

The driver gives me a look. Several minutes of silence pass before he speaks. He surprises me when he abruptly begins again. He says:

I THINK YOU'RE about to be ejected out of here and thrown into a parallel universe. For a long time I wondered what that would be like. For a long time I felt like an astronomer looking up all her days and nights yearning to know how many corners the universe held, and in how many were there beings fighting over power and fighting over access to pleasures and comparing theater experiences and writing history books and poems and fashioning devious and subtle prisons for one another and efficiently murdering and healing one another—in surprising efficiency or in surprising incompetence, given the graveness of their tasks. And you are about to go where I often wished to explore, except I no longer envy you or even pity you or think it will be an exceptional adventure. Instead I think all the constructions in all the universe's various corners are really the same. Lucky and unlucky ones might live in disproportionate numbers but in time, everything is evened out yes everything is evened out.

The driver pauses and then he says, Let me tell you about a construction I've made all on my own. At first it might seem strange, perhaps even insane, but in fact the more I've lived with it the more I think it might be universal or somehow this construction mirrors all the other constructions. It has to do with two stories I read on the internet. The first was an obituary, a small obituary, about an engineer's suicide. He was Ukrainian and a manager for many many years at the power plant in Chernobyl. He'd just begun his career when the disaster struck—and in fact he was not working that day. Even if he had been, no part of the disaster—which occurred in a reactor for which he had no responsibility—could be said to be his fault. He was blameless and in fact was often cited, so said the obituary, for his meticulousness, for the care taken in every detail within his purview. After the disaster, though he was of course pained and devastated, he stayed on and worked intensely on the repairs and on the plant's re-opening. For many years afterward he went to work and diligently carried out his duties, which required some skill but even more than skill they required consistency and follow-through. There was a photograph of him. He looked thin and strong, wiry, a bit like the young Lê Duẩn or the filmmaker Andre Tarkovsky. For years he worked diligently and then one Sunday he hung himself from a rafter in the dining room of his modest home.

The other story I read is about a South Korean scientist who had a roller-coaster career because he'd made some legitimate breakthroughs in genetics and, for a while, was considered one of the top minds in his field during a moment when there was considerable competition in the creation of human embryonic stem cells—and he did it, he accomplished this, or so he claimed. He'd won the race and his team crossed the finish line, so to speak, by being the first to publish a paper in *Science* magazine saying they'd done it through cloning. For several months he was a national, and even an international, hero. But then, slowly, it was revealed that the experiment was a fraud, that he'd faked the evidence, that he was a cheat. It was a terrific scandal. Later on I believe he recovered, at least somewhat, and with the help of some sentimental businessmen he re-established himself as a researcher, hobbled of course, at a second-rate company, nowhere near the heights he'd been before, a superstar, but working hard nonetheless, hoping one day to make a legitimate discovery that might in some way make up for his prior act of iniquity.

The reality of these two figures is not important to me, says my driver. But I started picking them up, so to speak, and started turning these two over and over, like they were interesting jewels or delicately made figurines. And I started to create a space for them, these two, the engineer and the scientist, says my driver.

In this construction they live right next to each other. In the morning the engineer wakes up and goes to work in the rather labyrinthine corridors of the Soviet-era power plant. There it's clean but filled with somewhat out-of-date technology — still perfectly viable, everything in working order, but the plant is outmoded by a decade or half a decade. And, similarly, in the morning, the scientist walks through the rather labyrinthine corridors of *his* laboratory — but his equipment of course is all very state-of-the-art. Everything is immaculate and at the very cutting edge of possibility, gleaming and antiseptic and pure in its efficiency. I watch them, says my driver, in their respective environments. Sometimes the differences are what's apparent.

The monolithic and slow-changing apparatus of state-controlled technology on one side and on the other the ingenious and constantly morphing and adapting perfect face of capitalism's research and development. How could they be further apart?

Yet more often it's the similarities that I notice. They're both very sensible and disciplined eaters, my scientist and engineer, and in the morning both have a small piece of bread or maybe a bowl of porridge or oatmeal along with a glass of juice and strong tea. In this world that I've made for them they both rise early. I imagine the engineer is a bachelor, rising early and staring out at morning's dark-blue shadows, drinking his tea and maybe recalling — why not? — a few lines of Pushkin. My scientist on the other hand is married. The scientist and his wife rise together, also very early, and they quickly but also gently begin their day together. The wife serves him his breakfast. His mind is already swimming with the day's calculations and with arraying and sorting through the methods and means by which his immaculate laboratory can make the material world reveal its secrets. Both my scientist and engineer do not taste their breakfast, their tea, until near the final moments of the meal, until the last sip or bite when somewhat automatically if not also miraculously they become aware of their setting and both think: How delicious! And the engineer savors his wonder; his whole being, unconsciously and consciously both, entirely, is grateful for his existence. A bare moment of everyday sublime for him. It's just a moment however and then he puts his cup and dish into the sink and hurries off to work. For the scientist this last taste makes him look up at his wife and erupt in some formality, almost every morning some stiff version of it, which endears him to his wife. Something like: "Thank you for such a tasty breakfast. Now, I must be going."

Abruptly my driver stops talking and reaches into his pocket and brings out a pack of cigarettes. He offers me one. It's a luxury I haven't seen in a long time and I hesitate to take it. Go ahead, he says, they're stolen from the house of an elite dogfucker in the city — so they're especially delicious. At his own insult, my driver erupts in a loud, sustained laughter. I take a cigarette and light up. He does the same. They taste different, almost as if they were laced with some other drug. The driver then continues.

On their lunch breaks the scientist and engineer, says my driver, take their lunches to the same park... Not always, says my driver. Not even usually, says my driver, and in fact most days the scientist and engineer skip lunch or wolf down something at their desks. But every once in a while, the first warm spring day maybe, they decide to take their lunches in the park. Magically, says my driver, the days that the scientist takes his lunch in the park always coincide with the days the engineer takes his lunch in the park. My driver smiles saying this.

What I'm reminded of, my driver says, when I picture these two in the park, sitting perhaps at facing benches or even sometimes on the same bench, is romantic coincidence. Like in movies and novels. And I think of my engineer and my scientist like childhood sweethearts or maybe twins separated at birth, who are unaware that they've moved to the same city or that they travel in such closely overlapping circles. How touching the potential of meeting is! How tragic that it never comes. The scientist absent-mindedly eats his roll of seaweed and rice. The engineer nibbles on a potato-filled dumpling. They think of powerful unseen phenomena: hurtling atomic wrecking balls and spiraling chains of protein. One's mouth runs dry. The other stares distractedly at a cloud or a bare leg. Sometimes they think of their government and countrymen. Sometimes they picture themselves in bed at night and consider what they look like sleeping.

EVEN THOUGH his cigarette is good and even though he's saving my life by risking his own in my escape—my driver is starting to annoy me. His effete imaginings are exactly what's wrong, I think, with the intelligentsia—so called. While he's playing his made-up games there are, I think, the death camps. I think of the police, of the constant preparation for war, of the famines, of my policeman. I take another cigarette from the pack. The driver smiles and nods giving his unasked-for permission. I think of the beloved president, of the police. I think of my policeman.

I THINK of my policeman. He was the local guy, not a specialist brought in. I was for once glad for our provincialism, happy my crime didn't merit a more immediately lethal or more specialized response. In order to control my rage and my helplessness and my fear—I latch on to our coincidences, the things my policeman and I have in common. As he takes a rubber hose to my legs and back, as he cracks a rib and smacks my face, as he prods me with his shockstick and my organs burn, and as he convinces me of my imminent murder—I note that we must be the same age, that we were most likely both poor students at our elementary schools, which surely were similarly grim and obscene, and that we both—like everyone else—grew up hungry and so constantly terrified we often could forget that we were.

This only helps so much however and I cry out, miserably, "I'll kill you, you son of a bitch." Which is a mistake because he hits me even more viciously and then I black out.

S OMETIMES, my driver says, late after work or early on a weekend morning, my engineer and scientist decide to exercise. They are not poets, my scientist and my engineer, says my driver, they do not in other words forget or discard their bodies. And occasionally they suddenly remember, their bodies remind them, that they should run or lift or bend, that they need to break a sweat.

The engineer prefers lifting weights—a soviet series of maneuvers he's learned in his army days. He grimaces and lifts, and during his resting minutes he feels something metallic released into his bloodstream, as if shaken or squeezed from his muscles. He breathes and thinks to himself with customary weariness: I'll be dead some day and none of this will matter. Then another set of fifteen. The scientist prefers the swimming pool. So several floors below the engineer, in the gym's basement pool, the scientist plunges into barely heated waters. (A sprawling complex, this gym, says my driver, tapping his temple with a finger.) The scientist flutters through the water, then he cuts it into blocks—swimming but without grace, a mechanic. In his mind is only the countdown of a self-prescribed series of laps, nothing more. Or, if so, only the vaguely autonomic commands: glide, stroke, breathe, glide, stroke, glide, stroke, breathe.

It's in the steam room, after their respective workouts, that they meet, or rather it's where they don't meet, says my driver, but where they commune in closest proximity, their ignorances leaning against each other, permanent strangers. I like to think of them here, the steam obfuscating what in any case is unknowable, that is, their faces. Sweat pours off them. They sit and look at their glistening bellies and the wiry nest of their pubic hair. One jostles his nuts to a more comfortable position. Someone sighs loudly. All of a sudden, says my driver, a quiet miracle happens. My scientist and my engineer merge into one being.

His face and body are hidden by steam and his consciousness is dumb from the erasures of exertion, but I've no doubt of this miracle, says my driver. Behind the white curtain of steam there is only one man where just before there were two. And then, says my driver, just as suddenly the moment of congruence is over. First the scientist (or maybe it's the engineer) leaves the steam room and then the engineer (or perhaps it's the scientist).

I'M FALLING asleep during my driver's monologue. I haven't slept for days. I know I have to stay awake but my driver's story is lulling even as it doesn't seem to make much sense. I catch myself dreaming about other things: my sister and my policeman. Then I snap back. Every once in a while I light up one of his dog-fucker cigarettes.

My policeman pours a bucket of cold water on me to wake me up. "So you're going to kill me, are you?" he asks. "No, no," I say, "I didn't know what I was saying. Please forgive me." I beg. My hands are bound behind my back and stretched awkwardly onto a table behind me. I'm forced into a squat. It's a painful position. He slaps me several times, almost gently, and then without warning slams the rubber hose down on my bound arms. I feel my right shoulder dislocate and a sharp, sickening hurt signals throughout my body. Quick cycling aftershocks of pain echo through a scream I only become aware I'm making after I begin it. I snap awake in the car finding myself in a cold sweat.

EVERY two or three months, my driver continues, the engineer and the scientist decide to take a weekend holiday. They're both, of course, nature lovers, says my driver, and they like best of all to take long hikes in the small nearby mountains and forest valleys. What best friends they could be! exclaims my driver, unable to help himself any longer… On the same overcast day in late autumn they both decide to take a hike. They both think: Perhaps a long walk through the woods will clear my head and provide some inspiration. And, they both think, I'm in such a rut. I need some inspiration, think my scientist and my engineer, says my driver. The leaves have long since changed color and fallen. The paths are relatively empty. Can you picture it from above? asks my driver. Can you see small mountains around a gulley through which crawls a thin, cold stream? The trees all leafless. And two moving spots: the green, down-filled jacket of my scientist and the striped sweater (a gift from his mother) of my engineer navigating the terrain with apparently no degree of gravity on each other, no attraction or repulsion, two atoms from different universes pinging past each other unawares. Like they say abroad, ships, says my driver, passing in the night.

And at this my driver laughs tremendously — an outburst of hysteria that soon devolves into a sputtering, hacking cough of dogfucker smoke.

At first, my driver eventually continues, my scientist's and my engineer's minds are, as a matter of course, distinct and distract-ed and taken up with the gritty magnitude of their daily trials. The engineer is motivated, is haunted, by the national memories of the disaster. He barely admits it to himself but he thinks he is doing noble work — harvesting energy for the collective, helping in his small way to sustain the great experiment of equality — and he struggles to maintain the corroding and crumbling plant with the drips and drabs of support the state sends. He is constantly looking over his shoulder at Entropy, who ruthlessly shadows him — it's like a nightmare — and he knows he can never outrun the disaster, but wearily and with heavy knowledge he knows he won't be able to stop trying. The scientist's mind is, in its own way, also beholden to the state. He so wants to succeed, to make the breakthrough—not for his own glory (he alone, the scientist thinks, understands it's not for his own glory) but for his nation's. So he tells himself. And success is so close, so temptingly, seductively close. He sees, in the abstract, how it should be possible. It would be such a relief if he could answer all those hopes with actual accomplishment… And these thoughts of my scientist and my engineer, says my driver, hover over them and are sifted by the denuded branches, blown by a cold wind across the valley and up the low mountains, and they intermingle with the rustle and crunch of their steps breaking through the forest floor of dead leaves and with the repetitive view swelling and passing as they walk of white birch and red pine, with the unbroken gray sky above them—until my engineer and my scientist are again indistinct from both each other and from the forest so that they become united in a timeless, spaceless motion. And if you were looking down at them as I have, says my driver, and had been watching carefully as their thoughts turned from particular things to be absorbed now with only hiking, then you too might not know how intimate the world had suddenly become… until, like my scientist you found yourself back in your sedan on the highway home or, like my engineer, brushing his teeth before bed, says my driver.

IN A DREAM my policeman seems to have my sister's face, which is odd enough that I realize I am dreaming. I decide then that I want to establish facts closer to reality with the intention—

a dream-fogged intention to be sure — that this will end my dreaming and wake me up. So I struggle to examine my policeman's face more closely, more intently, and I remember that my policeman's face had something very distinctive about it, namely a coarse, bushy mustache. In fact it is another thing my policeman and I have in common, a rather unique thing. I had begun wearing, so to speak, this mustache several years ago inspired by a Hong Kong actor in one of the rare foreign films that showed in our country. As my policeman is beating me I try to stare at his face with some vague intention to never forget it, to seek some vengeance upon it. But as he is beating me (hitting me with the rubber hose, whispering repeatedly, "For life, for liberty, for justice"), I have the thought: How odd. We both liked the Hong Kong actor so much that we both began wearing the same mustache.

MY DRIVER shakes me awake. "Here you go," he says "What's this?" I say.

"It's a change of clothes and a wig. We've arrived at the handover. See across the street there? That's the train station. Go change in the bathroom. Someone will find you."

I take the small package he's handing me and get out of the truck. I look at him through the window. I think he's a fool and am about to tell him so, but when I see him sitting stiffly behind the wheel, just another fellow bumbler, I forgive him. "Thanks," I say.

"Good luck," he says and drives off.

I make my way to the station. In a bathroom stall I open the package and find a field-hand's outfit—similar to my driver's: a broad-rimmed hat, a pair of prescriptionless glasses, and a shaggy, dirty blond wig. When I emerge from the bathroom I hope I can pass as one of the bumpkins that seem to be loitering in the station. I'm a little at a loss as to what to do with myself so I take a seat on a bench. A short while later a wealthy-looking woman approaches me.

"I've got you next," she says just like that and, "Follow me." We head toward the tracks to board a train. "Go fetch the bags," she says loudly. She points to a plump suitcase that I dutifully handle. We arrive at a private compartment and sit opposite each other. She hands me my ticket and advises that I should pretend to be sleeping when the conductor comes. I close my eyes and comply.

When the conductor does come I've actually fallen asleep. I mumblingly pass over the ticket I've been given with little idea where I am and none as to where we're heading. He hands it back to me.

After he's left our compartment I open one eye. The rich woman says, "Get some rest. You look tired." In fact I'm exhausted and the rumbling rhythm of the train is convincing lullaby. I see we're on the coast. I can, through drooping lids, see past a short sweep of trees to the water. It's late morning and the sun is yellow and warm on the landscape. Later on I'd realize this was the last I'd ever see my country in daylight.

I sleep for hours. When I wake up there's a dinner tray in front of me. A small feast has been arranged on our compartment's table: seasoned rice, thick chunks of pork in a stew, raisins in yogurt, a bowl of pickled seaweed, sugarcakes and mint tea.

I devour it and gradually become aware of the train's wobble and thrust. I look up at the rich woman. She says:

W E'LL BE there in about an hour. From there one more person will take you. It'll be by a small boat. A ship has agreed to meet you in high seas and take you on board and out of the country.

I don't actually exist. At least according to the state. We're traveling under stolen identities of course. Do you like imagining other lives and other worlds? Me neither. I find myself overwhelming enough. Which leads me to my story. I was a philosopher. Do you know what that is? No, of course not. It's a heretical art form now rarely practiced. The state claimed it decadent and a capital offense. Ah, you've never experienced it. The best I can do to describe it is to call it the regular rounding up of feral but cowardly dogs who tongue-kissed you for hours. If you had an affinity for it, it could be delightful. If not, it grew tiresome quickly — and in fact the art died less from state intervention than from lack of interest.

But I was found out. A cold winter afternoon. The sky turning purple. I was at the kitchen staring at my door as if I knew what was going to happen.

Do you believe in otherworldy things? I'm a skeptic, except. On occasion there have been strange and pivotal coincidences.

I was staring at the door. A cup of cold tea on the table. A pen in my hand thinking to write something down and a blank piece of paper in front of me. Staring at the door.

They were outstandingly silent. None of the boots crackled on the frozen ground. Or maybe I was distracted. The door, along with the entire small house, by the way, I'd built myself. Poured the foundation, chopped down the trees, planed the wood.

They broke down the door.

With a battering ram and an ax. It's ridiculous because of course I would have answered the door. A polite knock would have done. Quite literal the symbols. And bombs blow you up dead. They could have approached my little home and knocked or demanded, and I would have opened up immediately with no resistance. What could I do? I was living alone in the country in a rustic house of my own simple design and construction. I was sitting there, staring absently at it when the door exploded inward. The state, the state. I'm not even sure the door was locked.

They transported me to the camps. I won't go into detail. Even at that time I knew that parts of my body weren't entirely mine. There are no inalienable rights. Anything can be taken from you. Memories, sense of self—all for the taking. I entered sub-humanhood. Where I would remain for a long time. The unseen and forgotten. The trial! You're hilarious, hysterical… Accused by the living dead, judged by the living dead, sentenced by the living dead, jailed by the living dead. Transformed into the living dead. A bureaucratic ballet of corpses for no one's benefit. That is, a necropolis. So no hope there. Except the informal, random beatings were like kisses compared to what came later.

Which was a hell. Everything deadly and terrifying—just as you've heard, just as you've imagined, if you've bothered to imagine, if you've bothered to listen, if you could stand to. I won't describe it. I'll tell you of the people I met there.

I met a man who told me he'd run a bicycle shop. He said, especially when the weather was getting warm, the thing that most pained him was not being able to go on a bike ride. He sobbed at night because he felt ashamed and perverted that this was the thing that grieved him most. He died in the camps.

I also knew a man who was a musician and who loved to perform even if it was in the bumbling and corny marches of town parades. He was a trombonist. He confided that though he loved music, his real ambition in life was to be successfully in love. He'd tried therefore many women. He smiled as he said this. So far, he would tell me with a shrug, no luck. And he seemed genuinely disappointed. One day he decided to stop eating, and then they beat him to death.

There was a woman who so missed her two little girls (who had also died in the camps) that she pretended two other prisoners were her daughters—and talked to them, scolded them, advised them as if they were. Soon these two also died and the woman just picked two others. After a while people refused to speak to her but she simply addressed everyone by one of her daughters' names. For her the whole world was populated only by her daughters. By the time I left the camp she was still alive and more or less tolerated.

Here's how I got out. Another person's story. We were very different except oddly we looked the same. We could have been twins. This is what drew us together.

One morning I awoke as usual on the cold concrete floor of the dormitory. They were bringing in new people. The first days are the toughest in the camps. You don't know the routine. You keep expecting all you see — the skin and bones masquerading around as people, the pitiless beatings, the wounds suppurating, the freezing cold, the absurd and obscene death doled out with numbing generosity — you expect all that to be temporary. What malicious force could so wrestle with its own logistics as to keep such a hell in order? Impossible to imagine.

I don't know how we fell in together. At the time, though it seems odd now, no one, least of all us, recognized our affinity, our near exact resemblance. It may have been during some forced march or when standing around for hours in the cold or while gulping down some rancid but rare meal. In any case we started finding each other, even seeking each other out. I quickly noticed she was given a certain amount of special treatment. She was starved and tormented like the rest of us, but she was spared the more severe tortures. At first I wondered why, but gradually she told me her tale.

She'd been a film actress abroad. She'd starred in a string of sappy melodramas that had been huge successes. In fact the beloved president saw these films and became a fan. Which is how her troubles began.

The beloved president, who fancies himself a cineaste, wanted this actress for his personal stable. He suffers from delusions of filmmaking grandeur and thinks the actress will be the perfect spark to set blaze his movie-making fire. So he conspires to kidnap her.

One night, after the premier of her latest film, the actress is seen leaving a party and getting into a limousine with an unknown man. She's never seen in public again. As soon as she's inside the limo she's chloroformed and hooded. She's taken to a private jet and further injected with a sedative. A day later she finds herself in a sterile hotel room.

So began the actress's nightmare.

Henchmen, ministers and party heads, who were unctuous and skilled at seeming submissive when actually they were ordering her around, came to tell her about a great man, The Great Man, our beloved general, our dear leader—who wanted, she should be thrilled, to meet her and have her star in a film he'd written just for her. But she refused. At first she was simply in shock, but then she became outraged. She was an internationally known *star!* They had no right. She wasn't going to act in any seventh-rate film written by a petty tyrant hack! Et cetera. She had no idea where she was. They beat her and isolated her and threatened her, but still she refused. The last straw for them was a dinner with the beloved president... They'd tried to dress her elaborately for the dinner—though she refused to wear any of their make-up. She claimed, proudly, that she'd nearly clawed the hairdresser's eyes out—and after that, they'd just left her, naked and precisely beaten, on the floor, the evening gown on the bed. On their way out, someone whispered a quick threat. This was her last chance—and she was luckier than she knew. There was a simple coldness in this last remark that made her, finally, stand up and put on the dress.

By the time they came to take her to dinner, she was suicidal. At first opportunity she was going to lunge, to knife, to kick, to hurl—whatever it took to kill or to be killed.

But she continued to underestimate them. Three guards escorted her downstairs and stood behind her seat at a long, elegant table. There was no setting in front of her, no food or goblet to hurl, no knife certainly. The beloved president came in eventually—a chubby, average-looking man. Unlike the posters' image but more recognizable from them than she'd expected. He sat too far away to even spit at, however she suddenly tensed to make her attack. The guards understood what she was up to immediately, and she felt two hands fall heavily and unmistakably on her shoulders. No words were said. He just looked at her and made a dismissing gesture and the guards escorted her out. She didn't even think to scream a curse at him until it was too late.

She was sent to the camps shortly after that.

The actress and I, continues the rich woman, spend two years together there, and in that time we come to know each other very well. We notice that we start looking even more alike, until we finally become indistinguishable. Everyone thinks we're twin sisters—except the prison guards, who only think of us as numbers.

WHILE THE RICH woman is talking I recall my destination. After our parents died we were put in an orphanage run by at first the church and then, after the war's armistice, the state. We were split up, I still don't know why, and my sister was adopted to a family abroad. Beginning directly after our separation, I've talked every night to my sister telepathically before going to bed. I also meet her in my dreams. When my policeman with the mustache was beating me, when I passed out, I asked my sister where she was—and she named a glamorous foreign city. It seemed a particularly impossible destination, but it turned out to be, nonetheless, impossibly, where I find myself now heading.

Some nights before bed I would ask my sister, How do I know you are real or if you are still alive or if you remember me? And my sister answers only with silence—and between us this is a perfect joke.

ONE DAY, the rich woman continues, the guards come and take away the actress. I torture myself thinking the worst possible thoughts. But the next day she comes back.

She says the beloved president has written another film script and wants her to reconsider her position.

In return he will release her from the camps and give her the relatively luxurious options afforded the political elite: relaxed travel restrictions, her own house with servants, and the highest-quality food possible in our famine-stricken nation. Of course she'll become a different kind of prisoner, but it would be a paradise compared to her current situation. I tell her she shouldn't turn it down. The actress tells me she's negotiated my release along with her own. I am to be a servant in her house, a maid. To me, it's a miracle—but there is a condition. She won't do the acting. She refuses to act for the beloved president. She tells me I have to do it. She asks will I do it? Will I become the actress so that she can become the maid? I say yes without a second's hesitation.

The movie the beloved president wants to make is, I'm rather surprised to discover, a kind of science fiction film as well as, I'm not at all surprised to discover, a political allegory... In a sprawling, vertical metropolis of the future, the population is divided into oppressed workers and factory owners. The son of the foremost capitalist is awakened from his life of privilege by a woman—the character I play. She acts as a kind of prophetess for the workers. She predicts an end to the workers' suffering, a revolution, an enlightenment. Discovering this, the chief capitalist invents a robot in the image of the woman to sow distrust and confusion in the minds of the workers. The robot-woman incites the workers to riot and to destroy the city's generators, which inadvertently causes a flood in the worker city. The workers now believe all their children are drowned. (However, the son of the chief capitalist and the woman have in fact saved all the workers' children.) Feeling betrayed, the workers now go on the hunt for the woman whom they believe so recklessly incited them to riot.

They nearly lynch her but at the last moment capture the robot-woman instead. After a climactic battle, the workers realize their children are still alive. In the end the capitalists and the workers are united in a pact based on the common good.

It's hard to describe why—the script is not uninteresting, lavish amounts of money are spent on costumes and sets, and we all try exceptionally hard to not disappoint the beloved president (not the least of all because we fear how he'll react to a failure)—yet we only manage to make a rather clumsy and boring picture. Of course this is a semi-secret—since every screening ends in a prolonged standing ovation and our so-called journalists are in a stiff competition to see who can heap together the highest mound of shit in praise of it. Nonetheless everyone can see it's a failure. And even the beloved president, after enough time has passed so as to not lose face, even he quietly withdraws the film from exhibition.

The great general never tries, after this attempt, to make a movie again. My own fate however has changed. I am now a recognizable face—and the same journalists who propped up the dear president's soft directorial ego also manage to enshrine me as a kind of political angel.

It is decided that I will anchor the nightly news.

The propaganda department comes up with the idea. In the movie I'd been the prophetess, a catalyst for revolution but also a symbol of hope and integrity. What better vehicle, so it is proposed, to sanctify the hopelessly skewed version of reality the state requires to prop up its weird religion.

At the time though, I don't see it so clearly. I'd undergone a strange transformation of my own during the film's production. I had found I enjoyed being a star, being a member of the elite. It isn't merely the luxuries—though certainly they helped—but it's the various temptations of power that finally corrupt me. These temptations are insidious but powerful, especially to me, a woman who had heretofore always been on the bad side of a blow. As soon as I receive special treatment I come to expect it, enjoy the buzz when entering a room and the subtle and unsubtle deferences that are made to me. The whole thing very quickly becomes intoxicating.

I report what they tell me to say, almost proudly, almost believing in the utopian social contract I hawk nightly.

Somewhere deep down, actually not deep down. Just behind the exposed skin of my eyeballs. Just there I know the truth. That what I am reporting is fantasy. Falsehoods. Lies. But as you know, in our country, in our time, reality is a flexible notion, an unimportant one, if we're being honest, compared to the notion of the state, which is another word for paradise. And even though there is a place in my body that knows what I am doing, strictly speaking, is *lying*, I also know that I want more than anything to live in paradise, to continue to live in paradise, to help construct and preserve paradise. That seems like a simple calculation. I'm not even in conflict with myself, I think.

My maid at the time sees this transformation. I mean my friend, the former actress. With a rising sense of disgust and terror she sees me change from the executor of a very important joke she'd instigated into the worst part of what she'd been thumbing her nose at. She tries to talk to me about it, but I, at first, deny it. And then I say she can't understand because she'd been born an outsider, couldn't see that we *live* in this world now, that there isn't anything else. And then I rebuke her and say she's become a traitor to the state.

She withdraws then. She sees that I've lost my mind. And she is frightened too that, in my hysteria, I'll incriminate her, turn her in.

Later on she confesses to me that that time, the era of my betrayal, was her most difficult. Even worse than being kidnapped and violated and imprisoned was this perversion and cooptation of her friend and sister into the machine that had kidnapped, violated and imprisoned her. She feels as if a weed or as if some kind of cancer had taken root inside her and intertwined inextricably with her guts and her bones and her heart. It would have been a capitulation at this point to kill herself. Surviving, enduring, was important, was the point, she told herself. But so was destroying this long-tentacled parasite that had somehow become part of herself. She had to destroy herself and she had to live. There was, she thought, no solution.

She goes to a witch. She is desperate. There are still witches. Like the poor and like soldiers and prostitutes, there will always be witches. She can't bring herself to confess fully to the witch. She can only say, My sister is sick. But the witch seems to understand everything. The witch asks her, Do you pray? My friend says, Never. The witch says, When you shit—

My friend interrupts, When I what?

When you shit, says the witch.

Yes? says my friend.

When you shit you should pray that your sister will be saved.

From then on, following the witch's careful instruction, my friend performs a daily ritual of exorcism. When the news comes on, when my face appears on the state channel my friend will go to the bathroom. She'll leave the door open so she can see my face. The sound will be turned low, but she can still make out my voice, speaking those lies. And she will shit. She will shit very carefully, as carefully as she can. It feels odd at first. She is skeptical, but she is also desperate. So she performs the ritual as exactingly as she can. She shits carefully and with all her body and mind and she keeps only one thought throughout: Save my sister, save my sister, save my sister...

AND IT WORKS. Not immediately but gradually I let a first dim then brightening horror illuminate my brain. Reality begins firming up. So then I find myself in a truly fresh hell, unspoiled and virgin of my awareness until then. I wake up fully, a sentient cog in the propaganda machine... I realize in a flash how corrupt I've become, how I've traded truth for favors.

Then I'm awake. Immediately and feverishly I concoct all kinds of plans, all kinds of vengeful schemes as well as public and therefore suicidal outbursts of protest—but in the end my maid stops me. She says we have connections and mobility and we can use them to discredit the state, to build up the underground, and to be righteous terrorists...

AND THAT'S what we've done, but I'm afraid too cautiously. Every moment I wonder if self-annihilation might not be preferable to this, a complicity too slyly subversive. My maid had thought, and I have thought, that survival was a type of victory, indeed the only available form of it, but I wonder if it isn't in fact a most fundamental defeat.

Sometimes at night I turn to her, my maid. Or she turns to me, her imposter. And we torture ourselves, each other, with impossible questions, asking if the state hasn't succeeded absolutely and made us our own jailers, and hasn't indeed made our every thought a jail. And, we say to one another, if this is truly the case, says I to my maid or my maid to me, then perhaps it is not a jail at all and we are actually in the paradise the state had long-ago promised and in truth has fulfilled, despite our ignorance — and we moreover suffer continuously and unnecessarily out of pride and foolish apostasy.

THE RICH woman then stops speaking. I look out the window and see that the train is pulling into an empty station.

This is your stop, the rich woman says. Someone will meet you on the platform. Goodbye.

Goodbye, I say, a sour taste in my mouth. I think the rich woman's justifications are even flimsier than my driver's. "Just kill yourself and be done with it," I want to tell her. But I just stand up and leave the compartment and get off the train.

I'M THE ONLY one on the platform and, after the train leaves, a beautiful quiet arises and comes over it, as if a fog. It's the middle of the night now and I pace the platform waiting for whatever that is going to happen next to happen, growing increasingly tense, working myself up once again to have a conversation with Lord Death, attempting to accept his intimacy but never succeeding, still very begrudging. Which means only that I am terrified. I pace the platform, unable to penetrate the broad murk that surrounds the station's weak arc lights. A man with a gun then emerges from the shadows.

It is my policeman.

I SHOULD JUMP off the platform and run into the night, take a desperate chance, but something—perhaps the rich woman's tale—stops me from running, makes the idea seem disgusting. I square off against him.

Before you do something rash, he says, you should know that I'm not here to arrest you. I'm your final chaperone, the one who will take us to the ship that is to take us out of the country. He lowers the gun. Follow me, he says, and turns his back to me and begins to walk away.

I suppress for the moment the urge to tackle and throttle my policeman. He still has the gun after all. I let him lead me through the station and into the night. We take a narrow path through some trees and come out onto a beach. We walk down the beach for an hour before coming onto a dock with a wooden rowboat. We row out to a designated spot where we are picked up by a ship calling itself *Flaming Creatures*.

While we're walking on the beach to get to the rowboat the thin sliver of moon only occasionally comes out from behind dark clouds. At that time he asks, What if I said this had been a long-considered plan to liberate us?

Give me the gun, I say.

He stops walking and turns to look at me. He shrugs and hands me the gun. It isn't loaded, he says.

I point the gun at the policeman's head. It isn't loaded, he repeats.

Click, click, click.

You weren't lying.

No, he says, a bit ashen-faced.

I take the gun and strike his head as hard as I can. He falls to the sand.

Get up, I say. He slowly rises.

I strike him again with the gun, a crack to the side of his head. He goes down a second time.

Get up, I say. Again he slowly rises.

I move to strike him, but this time he anticipates the blow and tackles me.

IT IS AN EVEN wrestling match. I'm hoping to kill my opponent but am injured and weak and have no training. My policeman on the other hand, while well-trained and relatively at full strength (aside from the two vicious blows to his head I've delivered with satisfaction), seems determined not to kill me, for us to continue together. He pants that I'm acting insane, that we are close to escape, that we are necessary for the other to be allowed out. I've lost the gun. I look for a rock to bash in his head, but there's only sand. Why me? I ask him as he tries to pin me down and as I do my best to rip out his eyes. He grabs me by the hair and takes me to the water. He throws me down and puts his knee on my back and thrusts my head into the water for a long while. He lifts my gasping head. Okay? he asks. I swear at him. He dunks my head again and lifts it out of the water. Okay? he asks… Okay, I eventually answer. He stands up and lets me rise. I then tackle him again and we wrestle for some time more.

# IV. SISTER

When it was proclaimed that the library contained all books, the first impression was one of extravagant happiness.

—JORGE LUIS BORGES

Hᴏᴡ I ɢᴏᴛ the job is an interesting story. Like all her hires, I was recruited. It was when my twin brother invited me to a party.

A self-help book my brother had secretly ghost-written was having a launch party in the old-fashioned pomp and gilt of the Hotel Europa downtown. Its publisher was projecting tremendous sales so had spared no expense. I'd no idea what I was walking into (my brother had called a few days prior, surprising me with an invite), and so when I arrived and saw that I'd misjudged the event's size and glitter by several orders of magnitude, I realized it was going to be difficult to get any time at all with my brother, the epicenter of the maelstrom, whose tuxedo'd point from the mezzanine balcony I could amusedly observe drawing the aim of scheming vectors and incurring trails of vaporous gossip. Also, I was painfully underdressed. So I was both relieved and delighted when, twenty minutes later, he spotted me and instead of waving or just blowing me a kiss, immediately made his way over.

My brother said, "I only have a moment and then I've got to go back to making this whole shit wheel turn, but I wanted to tell you about mom and dad. Did you know they died last month? No? Well I'd no idea either, but I received an auto-reminder from the lawyer that the inheritance had been direct-deposited. I haven't thought of them in years. No offense, but I barely have time to think of you. Ha ha ha. Ever since I found out I've been trying to remember things about our childhood. I think I remember some things, maybe a shape or a locale… Of course I remember being outcasts. That's practically all I remember. Did we play games? Were we good at school? Tell me, because I've forgotten, what did mom and dad look like? I can't remember. Just general facts: were they thin or plump? Tall or short? Do you remember their hair cuts? No? Drat. I think we should get together and talk about this. We lived with them for our entire childhoods, we should be able to at least recall their names, don't you think? Look around your place. Maybe there will be a photograph or some other clue. Oh and I have to give you your half of the money."

Someone, one of his handlers, urgently began calling his name and an arm appeared to guide him away. "Let's meet next week!" my brother cried out while being whisked away. "Call my secretary and we'll have lunch!"

Then he was too far away, and I no longer could make out what he was saying. The crowd had spontaneously lifted him off his feet and were now passing him over their heads back to the center of the party. He no longer was trying to shout anything at me but smiled a big grin and waved as he was shuttled in that odd way back down the stairs and back toward the deep and charismatic voices of wealth and power. I was happy to have gotten the promise of a date out of him. The bit about our parents was a little nostalgia, a meaningless sentimentality, but as it did the job of securing some time together, I was grateful for it.

After that interchange, I remember planning to only gawk at the trendy crowd of lusters and confidence artists for the duration of a glass of free Riesling, hoping to then go home to a cup of chamomile and my police procedural—when someone tapped me lightly on the shoulder.

I turned to see a woman with long grey hair that she wore noticeably and elegantly loose. She had on a silver evening gown with an ingenious cut that seemed to jut out of her muscular frame by mesmerizingly clear, spindly cantilevers. A strong and beautiful woman, I thought to myself. She said, "When I'm in a situation like this and I see all this individuated extravagance I —maybe it's the mark of a perverse nature—but I, I think how, simply, each of us will die. But not only that. Which in itself is just a kind of morbidity, but also that the humble or swollen, generous or rapacious egos so displayed, that each of these was born through an unlikely yet destined chain of events and so could, on one hand, be seen as simply one particular facet of a constantly changing shape."

"Huh?" I said.

And then the captain turned toward me, for it was her, the woman with whom I now sail. And it was as if my exact response had been the password to begin a very necessary, dangerous, and confidential exchange between dumb agents. We were vessels being used by listening-in and remote-controlling darker forces. She took a finger and rubbed the side of her nose three times in a particular way. I touched each of my earlobes, almost involuntarily.

She said, "If I had a twin, and I'm not saying that I do, I would say we grew up in a simple house, squatting on a hill that overlooked a debased island, one used only as a trash dump."

"Go on," I said.

"If this were the case and in no way am I admitting that it was, then I'd say our mother and father were examples of a kind of utopianist, a type of idealist or religious seeker. In short, they were drug addicts and debilitated. My twin and I (should those two referents signify any aspect of reality) raised ourselves eating handouts from the market women and making toys and tools out of the junkyard, which was an ocean that seemed to us then almost as infinite as the real, but was not, no not nearly."

"I see," I said.

"You see what?" the captain demanded.

"No, nothing. Please continue," I said.

The captain touched the tip of her tongue with her pinkie. I took out a pair of zebra-patterned sunglasses and placed them on top of my head. She said, "If this happened to have happened, and please understand I deny and affirm nada, squat, zilchy-zilch, then it may have occurred that my twin and I began experimenting, playing, fooling around with at first electronic equipment then computational devices and then daisy-chained elements and then nets within and without other nets and then highly personalized and only occasionally brought-forth, never-uttered languages. With this expertise, if one is to believe such a tale, an action I neither endorse nor condemn, my twin and I might have begun reaching out from our trash island to stroke the belly of far away commodity exchanges, purring stock markets, and deeply dreaming arbitrage centers. Twins of this type, in this manner of story, may have taken odd numbers from that ambush of bewildered and half-sentient financial tigers, unliving or savage or mystical or deformed digits buried inside calculations and data and spreadsheets never actually handled but whose shadowy existences were made necessary by other gravitational events, other more obvious and prosaic numbers closer to the minds of drone bankers. Twins of this sort, though it isn't in my nature to speculate on their existential possibility, may have corralled these iridescent integers into more worldly shapes so that they, the hypothetical twins, could, should they want to (should they exist to want to), purchase not only the entirety of their own debased island but fleets of archipelagos and pinwheels of peninsulas and infinite itineraries of isthmuses for, in short, these perhaps possible twins were now—had become—bandits of an extreme order and therefore godly rich."

We had moved to a quieter nook, off-center from the party. Our voices were low and we simultaneously and craftily provided up easy-going, happy countenances to any potential uninvited observers. Underneath I was growing excited. This was the drop-off, no doubt, the *hook*.

That is: I'd, maybe we'd, decided it was.

"And finally," the captain whispered, through smiling teeth, "these people in this terribly funny story I must have heard from who-knows-where, spent years looking into the infinitely resolving space of capitalist markets. They dove deep into pools made up of pure cipher. They danced on precipices made of solidified, special mush which pitched unquestioningly and perilously onto a galactic void. Such was their extraordinary adventure that these two—if such a two could be—lost their minds. Gradually their gray matter sprouted lesions and bunions and whorls and growths, an accelerated and spontaneous and unexpected response to what they'd seen and contemplated. A madness that allowed them each, for a time, to function, but a madness nonetheless. As proof note that one built a self-operating electric chair and died on that pessimistic throne watching movies he'd made looping on a jacked projector, while the other, should this funny *ha ha* joke I'm passing on from something I must have *hee hee* have read somewhere be taken to its *oh ho ho* inevitable conclusion, this other twin *ha ha*, she must have outfitted an extravagant ship to wander, oh yes, just to wander—yes?" the captain concluded, turning suddenly somber, "Indeed, yes, just to wander."

I burst out in a stage laugh, not as convincing an actress as I wanted to be. "Oh that's a funny one," I sputtered, "but tell me, ah this is cracking me up. But tell me, what became, I should really want to know, what became of the, of the twins, of their parents?"

The captain turned to the wall and hissed, "Long lost. Long long lost."

I nodded soberly with tears in my eyes and told her I accepted the job on her ship. The captain and I then quickly left the party by separate exits.

Mu!

On this leg of the journey we have, as usual, a hectic
schedule as well as a pedigreed and at times flam-
boyant manifest. Cultural programming is usually
the result of the captain's catholic tastes, and on this
voyage it includes PANOPTI-CON, the annual gathering for lovers of murder mysteries—a huge affair with
hundreds of fans, authors, booksellers and publishers.
My favorite, Edward Gray, a lesser-known but in my
opinion excellent practitioner of the genre, will be
(I squealed like a schoolgirl when I learned of this) in
attendance and reading from his new book, *The
Sorrows of Priapus*.

In addition to the mayhem of the mystery mob
there's an academic conference around the allegedly
Bhutanese novelist H. B. Dorji, an author whose works
have generated intense critical and popular interest
due in part to their bizarre manipulations of narrative
but perhaps even more so due to the author's absolute
refusal to reveal, other than her or his name, a single
iota of biographical information. Ironically, and as
expected, this has generated feverish speculation and
interest into Dorji's life story.

And lastly the ship will also be home to the world's first film festival of monochrome films. Though the captain's tastes are definitely wide-ranging, this event was actually proposed to her by YJ, our cook. An ardent cinephile, he's evidently curated a world-class exhibition as a small legion of film buffs, conceptual artists, and museum directors have, as a result, booked passage.

And I bet, Mu, you'll be amused to hear that the whole journey has, in addition, a heightened salacious aspect. The convention comes with its expected horde of mystery-writer groupies, and the Dorji group seems a truly horny bunch—even for academics. For all this ship's lavish outfitting, better sound-proofing could have been arranged for the walls! Fortunately the monochromists are, in comparison, rather monklike; and many of them seem to retire for the night geriatrically, just after dinner.

Love and kisses,
Oona


What I hadn't dared mention in my letter to my friend Mu'nisah was the odd sequence of recent events. A few nights ago I was suffering with my unfortunately chronic insomnia. It was a particularly bad bout and I'd decided, as I often do, to walk the ship, which is especially peaceful in the small hours. A huge equatorial moon had made of the sea a shimmering sheet of ridged opal, and I let my eyes pleasantly wander to all the sides of the horizon.

By breeze and acoustical accident I suddenly overheard the captain talking in a strange language. Looking down I could see her on the deck below gesturing to an oddly dressed individual. He was skinny, malnourished-looking, and wearing some kind of uniform made of, it seemed from the way it reflected the moonlight, a cheap polyester. His right shoulder was encased in bandages.

I coughed and the captain looked up and met my eye. She made a quick gesture. I understood she'd meet me in the library and that I should wait for her there.

Half an hour later the captain arrived alone. We went to my office and closed the door. She explained that the man she had been talking to was a political refugee and that we were providing him with safe passage.

"I'm going to put him in one of the small rooms near the rest of the library staff. There're so many of them that one more shouldn't be noticed."

"Who is he?" I asked.

"I'd rather not say. You'll have to trust me. I'm going to advise him to stay in his room. Please understand this is a matter requiring the greatest discretion."

I began to argue, but she cut me off saying she was exhausted and asked if we could discuss this the next day. We bid each other good night.

AFTER THE CAPTAIN left I went out of my office and through the endless dark-wooden rows of perfectly somber library shelves. I knew I wouldn't be able to sleep so I kept walking. My thoughts muttered along with the melody of the ship's bow ripping the dark waves' silky fabric. In time I came across a figure on an upper deck. Habit and discretion told me to pass him without comment—insomnia, as a rule, an antisocial disease, even or especially among fellow sufferers. But there was something about his stoop that made me pause, that appeared familiar. When he looked up and the moonlight revealed his profile in high contrast, my suspicions were all but confirmed. However now I was frozen, star struck you could say, and was unable to flee or approach.

He solved the problem by turning to me and saying, "You and I could be anywhere in the world, do you know what I mean?" He grinned conspiratorially.

I nodded and said, "It's a displacement, a pleasant disembodiment." His smile grew bigger. "It comes from the sea," I added, unnecessarily.

"Now I recognize you," he said, "You're part of the ship's staff." He gestured dramatically at the moon-brilliant waters. "That must be marvelous."

"I'm only a few years on the crew," I said modestly. "I, I feel very, um, lucky." I stepped closer and now I was sure. My interlocutor was none other than Edward Gray, the author of the Inspector Mush Tate detective novels.

"Especially at this hour," he said, "with the clank of the mawheaded and the balless gratefully slumbering. In the wee hours, we're taken away from ourselves and made contemplative." He gestured again. "Add that to the sea and we find ourselves in a very far world indeed."

I couldn't believe he spoke in the same purple prose with which he wrote his novels. I wanted to blurt out some affirmation of his celebrity, some word to say I *knew* who he was—and that I appreciated him—but I proved too shy. My deepest secret was that I was an aspiring writer. I had an idea and, while having not yet put pen to paper, I constantly daydreamed a serial involving a broken-down, boozing and washed-up woman detective who is forced into seeking redemption after her estranged son goes missing. She either cracks the case in dark heroic fashion or loses herself in the desperate alcoholic fantasy that she does. It would be unclear. Certain scenes I could see very exactly. Should I have blurted this out in my ten accidental minutes with Edward Gray? I did not.

The great man and I looked out over the moving waters. After a moment—during which I was both at peace and yet ached—he said, "Well. Good night."

"Yep," I managed to say. "You too."

I WENT BACK to my room and filled up my little electric kettle. The water came out cloudy from the pipes but soon cleared. I made a cup of roasted corn tea and pulled down an old novel to glance through. It was one of Edward Gray's. In the passage I'd turned to, Inspector Mush Tate was making a beautiful, rich woman angry by accusing her of lying, which she no doubt was. In my mind I was both the hard-nosed Mush Tate and the desperate and glamorous woman. After the tea was cold I sighed and put the book down and turned off the lights and lay for a long time with my eyes open in the dark.

I *wake* UP to find myself alone on the cavernous ship. Everywhere I race, decks to bunkers to halls, no one is to be seen. I realize I must be dreaming and go back to my room to lie down.

I wake up and realize I've caught a strange disease. That afternoon I'd read about a woman in a magazine with a strange disease. She'd had a brain injury from a car accident. She was now convinced that everyone around her, including her mother and her husband and her children, were sinisterly disguised imposters. That these people looked and acted exactly like her familiars she never disputed, but she unhesitatingly concluded that they were not who they appeared to be... I find I've a variant of the same problem. Everyone I see, even though I can tell they look distinctly like other people, I'm convinced is myself. The ship is filled with me's, only disguised as strangers. I've converted the paranoia I'd read about into a narcissism, and in fact, once I realize this conversion is too neatly done, I understand I must be dreaming. So I return again to my quarters to lie down.

I wake up and find myself simultaneously in every room and hall and door and nook of the ship. My mind splinters and seizures trying to make sense of all that simultaneity, but when a moment passes and I realize that I'm not going to go insane from all the fractured input, I understand I must be dreaming.

A thousand me's return again and again and again to my room to lie down and go to sleep.

I dream of shooting myself in the head. I looked down upon my corpse and saw a stain of blood growing on the beige carpet. Why did I dream this? I wasn't very depressed and I didn't think I was so desperate for attention. It was true that I was lonely.

I *woke* up and, while brushing my teeth, I thought about my dream. I saw myself in the mirror, rabid-looking with toothpaste foam, and had that foolish-feeling revelation. Foolish feeling because I wasn't quite sure it was so simply true and yet I also felt it was. Yes, that's it, I thought. It's because I'm lonely.

I WENT ON DECK. Every morning the sun felt like a different place. Sometimes I thought it felt like Barcelona in autumn or Beijing in summer or San Francisco any cold, foggy dawn. Today I thought it felt like Montevideo in springtime, a clear and cool sweetness. I'd never stepped foot in any of those cities but I'd read a lot of poetry.

My plan was to find the captain and demand an explanation. I trusted her but not well enough to be kept entirely in the dark about a stowaway. When I got to the mess for breakfast YJ told me the captain hadn't arrived. A gaggle of Dorji academics had been scheduled to breakfast at her table, but she hadn't shown. It wasn't unlike her to be erratic or forgetful so YJ just in case had gone to her quarters to fetch her. There was no answer.

He had been on his way to find me when I saved him the trip by showing up in the galley. We immediately returned to her quarters. I opened the door with my master key (one of only two, the captain had the other), and we gasped to find a blood-colored stain on her beige carpet. YJ kneeled down and tested it with his finger. It was still wet and it was indeed blood.

We were a vast crew in terms of sous-chefs, housekeepers, bartenders, archivists, sommeliers, film restorers, projectionists, and carpenters. But in terms of security we had only YJ and myself. The captain had, it seemed like a joke at the time, deputized us last month and given us both a star-shaped tin badge. Did the captain know then that she'd be our first case?

"WHO DID THE CAPTAIN have dinner with last night?" I asked YJ.

"Two monochrome filmmakers. One who projects shades of black and another who works exclusively in white."

"Go talk to them. I've another hunch. I thought I saw the captain talking to someone last night."

"Who?"

"I'm not sure. I'm going to find out."

With not a little emotion we parted and promised to meet back at my office in an hour.

IN THE VAST ship there was a set of small rooms where the captain had indicated she would stash her stowaway. I headed there in a fury, convinced the figure I'd seen with the captain had taken advantage of her. Even though there'd been evidence pointing to foul play I foolishly didn't hesitate and went forth on a rush of adrenaline and anger.

I quickly located the narrow hallway that led to about a dozen small chambers. These weren't the palatial staterooms or even the sizeable quarters for the staff. These were purely functional compartments of little more than bed, desk, and small wardrobe, reserved for those token passengers who were with us only for a short leg: the never-ending turnover of lounge singers, string quartets, and jazz groups; the seasonal and region-specific sports instructors (hang-gliding and ping-pong and spelunking teachers); the chess grand masters who insisted on the austerity as part of their training; the fugitives from justice.

I pounded on each door before flinging it open aided by the master key. The first four rooms were empty. In the fifth a very good sessions guitarist, who in recent years was lost in a fiendish drug-fueled vortex, looked up from the bed. He was naked and a bag of chips rested on the sizeable mound of his belly. He began to shout so I slammed the door closed.

The next two rooms were empty, but in the following I found the man I'd seen talking to the captain the night before. He was sitting on the bed and gave the impression he had been sitting there for a long time. He merely looked up when I burst into the room like a riot. Something in his passive, steady posture robbed me of my momentum. "What did you do to her?" I said as menacingly as I could, but it came out limp.

He looked at me, tilted his head, and then spoke a slow repetition of sounds in which I recognized no cognates. I also noticed the bandage around his shoulder needed to be changed and that he'd been badly beaten in the not-so-distant past. We tried each other in a series of languages, and though he spoke it much better than I, we discovered our only mutual one was the Samoyedic Lithuanian dialect of Guarani.

I said—as menacingly as I could in the unpracticed tongue: *Where is the captain?*

He responded by saying something like *What are you doing?* though an equally valid translation was *What do you want?* or *What is your essential desire?*

I meant to repeat my question, *Where is the captain?* but might have been saying *How separate are the captain and myself?* or *Am I trying to kill myself or save the captain?* or *I don't want to die but I can't see how to live without purpose / the captain!*

He replied idiomatically: *Why are you asking me?* which could also be translated as Have you already searched everywhere? Or *Are you sure you've tried everything?* The most direct translation of his aphorism was something like: *Your complaints are weaknesses and have no business here!*

There was a tense moment of silence and then the stowaway said, in English, "My name is Noon. I want to go to New York City." Then in our mutual language he said, *The captain taught me that phrase.* Or he could have said *The captain wants this.* Or, yet alternatively again: *There are no captains—only death / New York City.*

I nodded and said the word for "captain" twice. Once in the affirmative and once in the interrogative.

He made his hand into the shape of a gun and shot me, making a childish sound effect: "Choo. Choo."

It dawned on me that this was someone the captain was protecting, perhaps even with her life. In addition, I had to admit to myself, the stowaway didn't appear to be in any condition to hurt anyone. I decided, at least for the moment, to stop considering him a suspect in my investigation. "Okay," I said in English, abandoning the Guarani, hoping that gesture would provide more clarity. "Stay, yes? Here stay! Here. This here," I said gesturing repeatedly with two flat hands as if pushing an invisible flat board down. "Stay, yes?"

He seemed to understand and what's more agree. I grabbed a pencil and piece of paper from his desk and scribbled a note to YJ that my hunch had turned out wrong and that I was heading back to the library. Getting up I gestured again for the stowaway to stay put and then left his room. Addressing my note to YJ in the kitchen, I chunked it into a nearby pneumatic tube and headed back to my office.

When I got there I found a note from YJ that the black and white monochrome filmmakers were leading a seminar that ended at eleven, and that if I got this in time I should meet him so we could interview them together. I looked at my watch. I would just make it.

Dear Oon,

Through an odd set of circumstances, which I'll describe in detail next time we meet, I recently managed to have a lengthy conversation with two filmmakers whose work I believe you admire: Wael Özseçen and Ginta Skalbe. I only have a moment to describe them, but they were an interesting set and I wanted to jot down a report while the impression was fresh...

Wael Özseçen was your typical Arab. Fat from their ridiculous diet of fried beefs and bananas, eloquent in a stupid and common way about global politics, and a mathematician in terms of his art—that is, all calculation and no emotion or risk. It was disappointing and the meeting, for me, revealed his entire lifework to be overly schematic and airless.

Skalbe was a Polynesian, specifically from Laos, and if you've ever met one of them you've met them all. She was obviously man-hungry and slatternly in that *Polynesian* way. There was a promiscuity in her eyes that foretold of disgusting diseases. Surprisingly though, she was the more interesting artist and spoke of her films movingly and in the most beautiful lies. It's the primitive lizard brain in these third-worlders that gives them the passion for the arts.

Anyway dear bro, I know you've a taste for these "experimental" works so thought you'd be interested. More very soon.

Love,

Sis

I liked to falsify my reports to my brother. My life was either too pedestrian so that I thought he'd lose interest or too worrisome (as in the current case with the missing captain), and I didn't want him to do something rash on my behalf. Not that I thought he was too concerned, just that his self-image as someone heroic might oblige him to do something dramatic. It was best, I'd decided, to send him short provocations, like my racist portraits, so he could privately tut-tut his little sister. Over the years I'd decided that was the optimum way to keep his attention without having him impede too forcefully on my affairs. I doubt he'd ever heard of either filmmaker.

The actual meeting with Wael Özseçen and Ginta Skalbe turned out to be rather consequential and happened like this:

WHEN I GOT to the kitchen to meet YJ, I could tell immediately that he was drunk. I couldn't blame him. This morning's scene at the captain's had been unsettling and led the mind to brutal conclusions. "Ah, you got my message," he said somewhat sadly when he saw me. As we walked to the quarters of one of the filmmakers where YJ had arranged our appointment, he gripped my arm in a both delicate and desperate way, as if unsure whether or not he wanted a rogue wave to take him absolutely out to sea. We walked like that, in silence, the entire way and then, just upon reaching the filmmakers' doorway, as I was about to knock, YJ collapsed to his knees.

I lifted him up, but he bowed his head and then began crying, performing an impressive human crescendo, and eventually shaking with sobs.

After some negotiation and embarrassed by the thought the two filmmakers might be hearing our pathetic conversation, I told YJ to go take a moment and pull himself together. I'd begin the interview, I told him, and he could join me if he felt up to it. He agreed. We shook hands rather formally, and he loped sheepishly off toward a bathroom.

A moment later I knocked and entered.

UNLIKE WHAT I had written to my brother, Ginta was not from Laos but was rather Latvian. She was in her early forties with pale skin and long hair accented with fashionable highlights. In hushed tones she was talking to Wael, who was perhaps a decade older with curly, salt-and-pepper locks and whose skeletal figure looked as if it had been punched into the heart of an enormous overstuffed armchair. He was Turkish but spoke accentless American English. They looked alarmed to see me.

"Where's YJ?" Ginta asked.

"He had to take care of something," I said vaguely. "He should join us soon."

Rising with some difficulty from the armchair Wael said, "Well, we might as well get started." They led me to another room furnished with a long conference table. At the table's far end I could see a brown, plastic cafeteria tray on which were set a syringe and several vials.

"YJ really should be here," I said cowardly.

"Yes, I agree," said Wael with a professional tone, "but we're terribly short on time. You must understand."

Sighing, I nodded and rolled up my sleeve.

"I love your blouse," Ginta said to me. "Where did you get it?" Her ploys to distract me from her needle preparations were obvious but nonetheless welcome.

"At a little boutique in Brooklyn," I said.

"I hear it's become very stylish," she said. And then, "Press this onto it. See. All done."

Immediately I could feel the drug begin to take effect. My hands felt heavy and the back of my neck tingled. "Okay," I said rolling back down my sleeve, "Why don't we all go into the other room and sit down."

"Okay," they agreed simultaneously.


AFTER WE WERE seated I took out my notebook. "Can you both briefly describe the theory behind your monochrome films?" I began.

Wael rolled his eyes. Ginta, however, responded without hesitation, "In my work I'm trying to bring our awareness to our looking, to see how we see. By projecting white—and not always the same white—"

"Never the same white," growled Wael.

"By projecting white," continued Ginta unfazed by the interruption and obviously well-rehearsed, "we study the self. By studying the self we forget the self. And so the barrier between ourselves and what we see is extinguished, and we are then enlightened by all appearances."

"My colleague," broke in Wael in a gravelly voice he cleared with a theatrical cough, "and I differ on some fundamental facts with regard to monochromatic film."

"To say the least," laughed Ginta.

"To say the least," echoed Wael without affect.

"And so what is your view?" I prompted, turning to Wael.

"My projections of black," Wael said after a moment, "which ironically are rectangles of the lightest shade in the darkened theater, are tempests in which the observer can see reflected his or her unspoken desires, not only dramas of patricide and incest but also our insatiable bloodlust and our bottomless vanity. And underneath it all, pervading all of it in fact, lies our indomitable death wish, which is sane, very sane, a wish for final peace."

"I see," I said.

"You see what?" they both demanded.

"Nothing. Tell me," I continued, "how did you manage to have a dinner date with the captain last night?"

"She invited us," Ginta said. "She wanted to get our opinion on a problem she was having."

"What kind of problem?" I asked.

They both hesitated, looked at each other and then at the table. It was Ginta who broke the silence. "The captain was growing increasingly concerned about you," she said.

"Me?"

"Yes. She said your behavior was becoming more and more erratic, that you were not getting your work done, not showing up for days, showing up drunk in filthy clothes, that she saw you go through periods of self-destructive promiscuity and that she suspected drug use. She said you spent days in bed. She was worried about you."

This information caught me by surprise. "Are you sure the captain wasn't speaking about YJ?" I asked.

"We're sure," they said.

I thought about it. It was true my attitude these past few months had not been ideal, but I didn't think it had gotten quite out of hand as Ginta and Wael made it seem. "But why did she speak about this with you?" I asked.

"Wael and I are well known in the field," Ginta said. "And I think the captain thought it might be time for an intervention."

"So you think I killed her?" I asked.

"The lock had not been forced. And you were the only other person with a key," Wael said.

"But let's not jump to conclusions," said Ginta.

"I think it's time," said Wael looking at his watch. "We're entering the peak zone."

We all stood up and went through yet a different set of doors and entered a small screening room. "We're going to show you some of our films so you can get an idea of our work," said one of them, I wasn't sure which.

I heard the two of them leave the small theater. The lights slowly dimmed.

THE SOUND of a pneumatic woke me up.

I was in my quarters in the middle of the night and wasn't sure how I'd left Wael and Ginta's theater or how I'd gotten back to my room. I opened the pneumatic tube and read the short note inside: "Come meet me in the HELICOPTER."

The HELICOPTER was the name of the ship's submarine, which was docked in a bay on the lowest level. I dressed quickly and headed there, knowing I should alert someone but wanting to confront what was there alone.

The submarine's hatch was open. I climbed down into it and took a seat in the main compartment. The hatch was made to seal remotely so I knew someone was at the controls. We launched.

I felt a mild anxiety coupled with an escalating thrill as I realized we'd left the ship. It appeared like a planet after lift-off, ineffably reduced. We began tracking a path below and beside it. I was relieved to see we weren't leaving the ship's region, still imposed upon by its gravity. We fell back a bit. At first the ship's hull grazed the top of the view from my porthole, and then our headlights lit up the frothy, bubbly wake of the ship's giant propellers.

A speaker switched on. A voice said, "In early adulthood, at our parents' funeral or just over dinner one night or maybe first breathed as a joke which gathered materiality slowly over time…"

The speaker in the HELICOPTER cut out abruptly and I only heard the hum again of the craft through the water and with fascination I continued to watch the bubbles churned up by the ship's giant blades. I thought the voice's narration was over but then the loudspeaker hissed a short prelude and it began again, this time continuing without further interruption. The voice was mechanized, unfaithful to its original sound, heard as if through a long and narrow tube. It might have been the captain or it could have been some abductor impersonating the captain. I couldn't tell. Echoing in the submarine's small compartments, the voice said:

IN ANY CASE at some point when we were younger my twin … brother Henry and I decided to split up. To go our separate ways. A thoughtless decision.

I mean by that not that it was a rash or an incorrect one but that we didn't comprehend it or evaluate it or understand its cause. We only acted.

He hopped on a plane to New York and I decided to take the slow boat down the South American coast.

Which resulted in an odd sensation. I'd never been apart from my brother and, to put it mildly, had become habituated to his reflection of my own thoughts. Or my reflection of his. Habituated to the echo and company of my brother. So when we split up, initially, the silence was deafening.

But I gradually got used to it, gradually absorbed this silence and allowed it to enclose me, a scary alien slime, a foreign and solipsistic environment. And eventually, I became used to it. It wasn't instant. The process took some time. And it began on that slow boat, of course much much smaller than our ship…

It was a coastal freighter holding at first several tons of PVC piping and then coils of copper wiring and then crates of film production equipment and then bolts and bolts of gaudy cloth. Its progress was tropical, leisurely, and forever interrupted by these exchanges of goods.

I barely noticed, having paid a tidy sum to the freighter's owner in order to sit undisturbed day after day on a banana crate on the deck and look at the slowly transforming landscape. My skin burned and blistered and then became weathered. I ate the same meal of fruit and salted fish and beans and rice twice a day every day. I appeared stolid and strange but inwardly I was trying to come up with a plan. Our parents were dead. My brother and I were no longer children. We were rich but had no real connection to the world except each other—a connection we'd both suddenly and mutually decided to sever.

I was thinking what to do with my life but nothing really came.

Day after day passed and instead of thinking about and concentrating on and solving my problem, the boat's languorous movement and the passing muddy scenery lulled me into a slow emptying out. I kept trying to come back to the problem. What am I going to do? What am I going to do? But each time the question turned flimsy and abstract—and tended to float away leaving me with only mundane and immediate ideas. Counting the hours until my next meal. Wondering what was to become of the cargo of soy sauce drums or plastic outhouses or solar panels. Watching the quick movements of the monkeys in the trees or the impatient or resigned shuffling of the crew and dockworkers or my own back as it ached or was relieved of ache by my shiftings or just the sky going from rose to cyan to a glowing umber then to grey then to black.

And, I've to admit, other questions hummed in the background or sometimes burst onto center stage unannounced: Where is my brother? What's he doing now? What's he thinking now? What were we together? What are we apart? Who is he? Who am I? It was a loud murmuring, a theater's indecipherable roar, which muted my other intentions. But these questions too, by some subtropical or aquatic spell, slowly also became airy and transparent and thin. Until they too almost faded to nothingness and there was left only the gentle swaying of the boat and the cries and jokes of the men and the buzzing and chatter of the jungle and the relative urbanity and bustle of the docks.

After traveling this way for months, up and down the coast, I found a certain kind of peace. At first it was a sweet, delicious sensation. Like water to a parched throat or a cold room to someone wandering a desert. An atmospheric feeling that was a relief to chronic pain. But then it became too familiar. And then I began to feel restless.

One day I got off the ship.

I went to the nearest town and took a room.

I sat on my bed with vague hopes but no notion or desire came that could point me in a direction. After a week of sitting this way it occurred to me that staying in the hotel room was, like staying on the boat, its own path—and the idea that I'd made a choice or set on a course disturbed me. I felt I wasn't yet ready. It wasn't yet time.

From then on I let fate and chance be my principles, ones I hoped saved me from hypocrisy and a false direction. I'd flip coins at forks in the road or throw dice in front of train time-tables. Nothing ornate. Simple procedures. I was careful not to sanctify my methods or fetishize chance itself as my new direction. The aleatory path, I knew, had its own traps. There was a limit to how much and how long I could rely on it, but I wasn't yet ready and wasn't imaginative enough to come up with any other stop-gap method.

Due to a succession of coin flips and dice throws, for a term I worked in the information technology division at a large company. I performed the job well and even enjoyed it. I was offered a promotion, but a coin flip decided I shouldn't take it. A few weeks later I quit rather abruptly, also from the counsel of a flipped coin. I didn't have to work, but the dice and coins kept pointing to various occupations. During that time I also worked as a hotel cleaning lady, as a dispatcher for a taxi company, a dishwasher, a finance journalist, a street-food vendor.

It was at the last job that I met Maxine. She was tall and thin-boned and wore her hair in an abrupt style.

I'd bought a souvlaki cart. (No one would actually hire me to be a street vendor so I had to outfit myself.) In the small hours of the night, I'd park my cart near a section of the city that had several night clubs. These were the less fashionable clubs that had popped up in a desolate district and where, I'd noted, there were very few all-night restaurants for the hungry and typically drunk after-hours crowd. My cart did a brisk business selling gyros, shawarmas, and fried potatoes in a sack.

It was a cramped and dirty type of job, but I came to enjoy serving the tired and hungry clubbers. They were silent and direct—young people eating out of need and not from any form of conspicuous consumption. Stopping at my cart was an unglamorous necessity. But I liked dealing with their directness. They seemed to me as if they'd left an exhausting religious ritual, which, of course, they just had.

Maxine was a manager of one of the clubs and would come out of her building periodically for a smoke break. She never bought any food from me but one day I decided (not by coin flip but from an agency inspired by Max alone) to talk to her.

Even though we seemed to have very little in common, we hit it off. Maxine was a fan of American cop shows and my total ignorance of them amused her. She would spend a long time describing the plot of one of them, almost to herself, as if the reconstruction of the story in her mind was a pleasant chore she was fulfilling for my sake. We fell into a habit. She would give me one episode per cigarette. Her only preamble would be to tamp her Pall Mall on the back of her hand and light up expertly. After a puff she'd launch into her summary: "So Stabler is waking up a judge to get a warrant, but he's worried about Benson who is deep undercover…"

After a few weeks of this, which amounted to a seemingly infinite number of episodes, I moved into her place.

One night Maxine came home and I was on my hands and knees scrubbing the floor. The tiles were black and white hexagons. She had a paper bag of groceries and placed them on the floor.

Another time we got dressed up and went to the orchestra — a treat we rarely allowed ourselves, though she always had the radio on or a record playing music. We were completely charmed by the red velvet, the chandeliers, and the conductor's stiff, quick arms.

Her mouth was always bitter with the taste of cigarettes but her cooch was salty and smelled of the expensive shampoo she used on her hair. We made love all day on Sundays or, during the week, after one of us would come home very late and wake the other. We'd be sweaty and grimy from the day or from the hours of summer sleep and the moonlight would make the sheets and our skin glow.

That's how I remember the time with Max, in a few sentimental scenes. It didn't last long. We both suddenly got bored and I broke it off because I got scared it would last or that it wouldn't last. I admit to thinking about her often ever since.

I moved into a hotel and was scared because I hadn't flipped a coin or rolled dice in such a long time, and it didn't seem like a philosophy I should just pick up and put down at my convenience.

I wandered the city less randomly than in a daze.

It was summer again and I constantly wore the same thing: an ancient pair of running shorts made out of some space-age glisten and a filthy black T-shirt. I wore uncomfortable sandals that made an annoying sound with each step but I endured them because it never occurred to me to buy another pair. At night when it was cold I wore a green rubber raincoat that stuck uncomfortably to my sweaty skin but which I preferred as it had a hood and made me a lumpish and anonymous figure in the night.

A dead space was mounting in my brain, a kind of frustration. It could have been that I missed Max and regretted our breakup. It could have been that I was angry at being paralyzed and that I felt lost since leaving my brother. I tried to stay calm, but as more and more time passed, outrageous thoughts kept beckoning.

One night I was crossing a cobblestone plaza in the weak light of a street lamp. As I set foot in the square I saw someone else enter on the opposite side. As we approached I could see it was a woman roughly my age, well-dressed and with a lucky-looking, haughty face. In the moment before we were closest I decided to try something. I thought of it almost that way, as an experiment.

A split-second after we passed I turned and, tripping her, gave her a hard shove. She fell forward, stunned. I pounced and took my open palm and smacked the back of her head with such force her noggin bounced off the cobblestone like a ball. She cried out and I then sprinted away, my sandals in my hand, barefoot—a raincoat-hooded, feral rodent.

I ran to the canal network that crisscrossed the city. At the water's edge, in the shadow of concrete slabs, I caught my breath and surprised myself by grinning. The next morning I was a little horrified but also intrigued to understand that terrorism could be an expression. I admit to doing it again twice more, in a more premeditated way, with a businessman and with a bitter-looking pensioner. With the businessman I used pepper spray and then punched him in his soft gut. With the old woman, I delivered two vicious slaps. Each of those times the satisfaction diminished and the horror with myself mounted and I stopped after those two, afraid I was becoming a psychopath. I nonetheless discovered there'd been something learned in temporarily embodying violence and rupturing all expectation.

I still didn't know what to do however and continued to persist in an ambulatory fog. I'd forsaken my hotel room and was sleeping in the shadows of the canal, the rubber raincoat becoming my only shelter. I ate, ordering with a fading nostalgia, from the city's hospitable scatter of souvlaki carts. I'm not sure how much time passed this way.

One day I found myself in front of an impressive façade I couldn't recall from all my weeks of wandering the city. I walked up an impressive angle of long and wide municipal steps to gaze at huge double doors recessed behind thick Doric columns. It was the city's library. I felt a great sense of relief as I entered, as if my anonymity, my prideful loneliness and my refusals were all appropriate here, had in fact brought me here.

After passing a series of apparently abandoned reference desks and sparsely populated reading rooms (holding a handful of dozing senior citizens and even fewer oily-headed students), after a few great halls and a discordantly abuzz café, I came to the library's stacks, which were uniquely designed as a vast network of honeycomb so patrons felt, at least I felt, like an insect, a drone, crawling over the world for something—a queen or a tomb or a morsel, I wasn't sure.

The initial feeling of relief, as I began wandering through the library's numberless rooms and infinite bookcases, modulated with one of terror. I was in the right place, but that place was only the empty space of the universe cruelly insinuated in fractal form by the endless spiral of helix shelves. The library didn't seem to have any hours. Or, no one ever bothered to kick me out. Libraries are, as you've no doubt discovered, a kingdom unto themselves. I'd already been used to sleeping with only my green raincoat as defense between myself and the city's weather so it was in fact an easy transition to sleep in a desk chair when—

T HE VOICE stopped and the small speaker in the HELICOPTER abruptly hissed out.

A moment later I felt the craft shudder and sway as it docked and as water was pumped out of the air lock. For a few seconds the main lights went out and the only illumination came from a string of pretty small white lights outlining the ladder, but then the whole bay was flooded as overhead fluorescents tap tap tapped on. I heard the hatch open. I climbed out and walked in a thoughtful silence all the way back to my room.

There, lying in my bed and reviewing what had happened, I began to be cautiously hopeful that the captain might be safe.

YJ AND I WERE eating lunch in silence the next day. I hadn't said a word to him about my adventures the previous night, and he was equally quiet, perhaps ashamed with his behavior outside of Wael and Ginta's. I cleared my throat to break the silence but was interrupted when the first of the bombs exploded, shaking the galley and indeed rocking the whole boat.

We rose at once and began running toward the sound of the explosion, which had come from the ship's aft. Alarms sounded and pre-recorded announcements came on directing passengers to their muster stations to be counted.

I was yelling orders to various crew members while racing toward the damage when the second bomb detonated several decks below us. I leaned over a railing and could see the smoke pouring out of a room whose wall had been pulverized by the bomb. I watched a charred wardrobe dribble overboard and suddenly sniffed the rank odor of burning plastics.

I wasn't immediately sure, but the thought occurred to me that the exploded room was that of the stowaway. I found myself bounding down the stairs and through miles of hallway—only to be brought to an abrupt stop, hammering against a firewall that had sealed off a wing.

THANKS TO the sprinklers, the state-of-the-art suppression systems and the bravery of the ship's crew, it took us less than an hour to get the fire under control. One member however did panic and launched two dozen loaded lifeboats. Thankfully the seas were calm, but it would take some time to restore order and even more time to figure out exactly what had happened.

Over the course of the next few days, even though no body or explanation was found, I became increasingly convinced the stowaway was dead. When, later, I asked the recovered captain, she shrugged and said she didn't know anything more about it. This was quite maddening, but as her expression at the time was unaccountably sad, I never pressed her further.

At the time of the bombing, shortly after it was clear the worst had passed, someone in the crowd handed me a note. I opened it and read, "Meet me in the SUBMARINE."

I told YJ where I was heading, saying I wanted to get an aerial view of the damage. The SUBMARINE was the name of our helicopter.

As I neared the helipad I could hear the blades already in noisy action. Through the helicopter's plastic bubble I saw that the pilot had on an elaborate helmet that made it impossible to identify him or her. I got in, and the pilot nodded and gave me a headset. I put it on and buckled in while the pilot flipped some switches and then pulled back on the stick and lifted the SUBMARINE into the air. I looked down with awe as the injured ship shrunk, two coils of smoke still flagging the bombed sites, and the ocean swarmed around it—dark with quavering glints of sharp light and now sparsely decorated with a small dotting of yellow lifeboats. I saw the pilot cough into her or his headpiece and heard a staticky analogous eruption come out of my headphones. The pilot said, "We'll repair the hull damage next week." The voice was familiar. I nodded. We then circled the ship a few times and the pilot said the following:

THE LIBRARY didn't keep any particular hours. Or, no one ever bothered to kick me out. I'd already been used to sleeping with only my green raincoat as defense between myself and the city's weather so it was in fact an easy transition to sleep in a desk chair when I needed to. It was far from crowded. I could go for a long time, it could feel like days, without seeing another soul. I wandered the stacks, which were uniquely designed as a vast network of honeycomb so patrons felt like an insect crawling over the world for something: a queen, a tomb, a morsel.

I made an advancement on my method. Coin flips and dice would guide me to a certain room, a particular shelf, and finally a single book. I could spend as long or as little time with the book as I desired, and if its contents aroused an interest I could explore the topic further. But usually I jumped from room to room, shelf to shelf, book to book. I read: *The Christian Book of Mystical Verse* by A. W. Tozer, *The Gold and the Glitter* by Juan De Ariza, *Restoring the Chambo in Southern Malawi: Learning from the Past or Re-inventing the Wheel?* by Mafaniso Hara, *Handbook for Typesetting* by Friedrich Bauer, *The Woodcutter* by Mahmoud Shukair, *How High is the Sky?* by Chi-Song Choi, *Advances in Numerical Simulation of Nonlinear Water Waves* by Qingwei Ma, *Malice* by Danielle Steel, *Believe It or Not: Why December Is the Best Month To Job Hunt* by Marshall J. Karp, *The Cost of Achieving Community: Pericles' Funeral Oration* by Jim Mackin, *Combat Leader to Corporate Leader: 20 Lessons to Advance Your Civilian Career* by Chad Storlie, *Earthlight* by André Breton, *Chinese Theories of Fiction: a Non-Western Narrative System* by Ming Dong Gu — and countless others.

I was wandering the library, searching and not searching, a question permanently on my lips, growing hopeless. At the vending machines one day I struck up a conversation with someone. It turned out he was a librarian, which surprised me, as I hadn't ever seen any persons that could be identified as such. He said the library had an innovative reference policy. Patrons didn't seek help from librarians, rather the librarians were trained in a special method of intuition. They tried to anticipate when a patron needed their help and only then did they approach. It was a controversial method when first implemented. People complained they were being watched, that their privacy was being invaded — but when it was understood that the librarians weren't observing patrons but simply sitting in chairs and waiting for "the spirit to move them," then the citizens of, it must be admitted, this rather religious state became quite happy with the new technique, which now can claim fairly universal support.

The librarian was an older man, fiftyish, with a muscular build and stone-white hair shorn into a very rectangular crew cut. We took our vending machine coffees and our vending machine food (which, incidentally, was quite good: a jalapeño chicken empanada for him, a peanut butter and apple jelly sandwich for me) and retired to a quiet table. He started telling me about his family.

He said, "We had a boy and a girl, twins. My wife and I were very poor and always busy but the two children took care of each other. They played well and would tell stories to one another. It was almost as if they were raising themselves... One day I listened in on one of the stories they were telling. I forget if it was the boy talking to the girl or the girl talking to the boy, but I remember being surprised, shocked even, because the stories I was overhearing were soaked in bloodshed. This was not the cartoon violence of storybooks. Their descriptions were filled with very real details of the most incredible sadism. At first I was going to stop my children and ask how they knew these things or why they were talking about them, but then I saw that while I initially thought they were laughing and giggling like normal children, I saw now that they had on very serious faces, very adult faces, and I thought that these weren't my children at all, or if they were my children they were also a kind of judge and advocate in final arguments and I realized it would be a grave mistake to interrupt or question them. I let them continue and went outside on the pretext of doing some chores. I couldn't hear them anymore. I could only see them through a window but as I got further and further away I was thankful to see they seemed more and more like my giggling and happy children again, more and more like they were playing some pretend game and just making up some story."

The librarian stopped speaking and then, after a moment, looked up. I slowly nodded. Now, I thought to myself, we were finally getting somewhere. I could feel myself preparing to give a detailed response to my newfound companion. Or, he was gearing up to perform a long monologue. I could see it in his face—that we were set to have a very important exchange. Our plates were evidence we'd become engrossed. His empanada lay almost untouched and I'd taken only a bite of my sandwich. Our coffees were cold. But before we could begin I saw that he was no longer looking at me. I was waiting for him to begin a tale, or for myself to start one, but then he pointed behind me.

I turned around and saw a young man standing there.

The young man said, "My name is YJ. It's taken me a long time to find you." And then he stared openly at me for quite some time, intently, gauging my features and, I later realized, searching for some resemblance to his recently deceased friend, my brother Henry.

Dear Oona—

How are you? Me? Just the same old
same old. But I'm keeping busy.
Thinking of you. Wish you were here.

Love,
Oon

# V. THE TWIN

By the interaction the two representatives
have become entangled.

—ERWIN SCHRÖDINGER

OON AND I knew each other through other people at first—his sister worked with an old friend of mine—and then we got to be friends on our own. We'd meet near an enormous oil painting of a tri-mast galleon in the entrance hall of the central public library. We wouldn't stay there; it was just where we met. "Noona, let's meet by the ship in the library," he would say to me. And then later it would just be, "Meet you at the ship." And then we'd take a walk. This went on for many years, well over a decade, until eventually Oon moved out of the city. Now we don't even talk on the phone or send letters. And yet for over ten years we saw each other every week. At first, when we started meeting regularly, I thought it would turn romantic. He was recently divorced and I was single, a long-time widow. But his divorce I think was still fresh when we began our walks, or I too much preferred being single. Probably more the latter as I think it's still true. Or, probably even truer still, we both recognized in the other an unrelenting distance that only allowed so much intimacy. Though we both valued the friendship — in fact I think for both of us it was crucial — nonetheless there was within each of us an inviolable domain. We might not have even known, at first, that it existed, a hidden mass influencing our system. But eventually we knew. And were co-opted into its veiling, into its protection. It was a question of survival. Which is a long way to say I know why I never pick up the phone and call Oon. And why he never calls or writes either. I mean to say I don't know why and I know why both.

One day as we were walking, he, or maybe I, said, "My friend killed himself. He was an old friend, one of my only friends, a close friend. But I don't blame him, not really. I'm not sure if his particular situation was intolerable but it was intolerable. I mean I'm not sure in what particular way his situation was intolerable but I'm sure it was intolerable in a general way. I mean in the general impossible way we all tolerate the uncertainty and the doubt and meanness and the selfishness."

It was a mild day, a perfect one for walking. The streets weren't desolate but also not too crowded. I responded, or he said, "Of course I totally disagree. I'm not unsympathetic but it was a tragic decision, deserving of pity. There are land mines and profound larcenies and divorce proceedings and all kinds of cruelty and humiliation of course — I don't dispute it! But the miracles to have faith in are the not-so-rare acts of tenderness and the lucky and instantaneous recognitions still possible."

"Please," he or I said, "Spare the rhetoric. The world is

drowning in such bullshit. All lies. All the most corrupting and acidic ideas, eating away at our relationship with the truth. Here, I'll hand you some more of it to combat your own. So we can distract ourselves while being robbed blind. How polite of us, how yielding! We even spare the thieves the effort of deception, of subterfuge. We provide that ourselves. Listen. Here is what destroyed him in the end, absolutely though indirectly. The science fiction story has come true. The machines we have built have finally outgrown us and have taken over—and what's more are harvesting our organs for their own sinister purposes. I mean the corporations of course yes."

"Oh, come on," he or I couldn't help it but say. "That's its own sentimentality. People are given work and food and shelter due to the complex chain of events you simplify into villainy. You're much more devolved than the people you see as dupes or even those you see as self-justifying puppet masters. Because your mind cannot fathom the complex plot, the infinitely varying story, the total story which you can never, will necessarily never, completely understand—in response you fake it. You make up grand narratives that reduce the world to heroes and villains, to victims and thieves. You're a child."

"Bravo!" we erupted, in a nasty sarcasm. "An eloquent defense of butchery, of venality. Also of product jingles and market manipulation and wage slavery."

To that one of us said, "Calm down. Am I saying no to anarchy? To personal liberation? Of course not. But at the same time you have to realize such a liberation isn't real, isn't actually possible.

Your rebellion can only exist in your mind and only if you have the strength for it. Otherwise you're the same as everyone else. In fact, let's be clear about this, one is always the same as everyone else, just luckier or less lucky. And the evolving mechanisms of power, the inequalities, the crowds of humiliated and stupefied, and the growing legion of suffering poor will always be there. And it will always seem corrupt and unjust and abject. And there is no end to it. And it is your attitude of protest that is actually the more childish because it pretends a defiance when actually it's a predicted and, in its way, needed behavior for the general state's survival."

We turned into a small city park and let our exchange linger for a moment and then dissolve back into the void from which it had erupted, not really an argument but more the repetition of happy, old habits. I bought us two lemonades since it was turning into a hotter afternoon than when we'd started out and also as it was my turn to do so. We sat at a metal table and our clear plastic cups beaded sweat in a refreshing-looking way. We looked toward the trees and not at each other as we spoke.

He or I said, "I don't know."

"Yes," I or he responded, "I agree."

We were in a popular spot on the edge of the park next to a wide traffic circle. We watched the swirl, our eyes and ears picking out the beautiful people, the stand-out choices of fashion, the tourists and street artists, the quick evidences of psychology, the foreign languages, the arguments.

"I don't know."

"Me neither."

He pulled out a small book of poetry and began reading. I was watching a boy assembling something; it looked like it was going to become a kite, which reminded me of playing with cicadas with my brother. I was conscious Oon and I would appear to any onlooker as old-marrieds.

"A few years ago," I said, "I felt like I was being followed, shadowed. At first I wasn't sure who it could be but then I thought it was my twin brother, one I had been separated from when I was very young. In those days whenever I woke up the dim, muffled residue of dreams held his face and his voice. He was in a repressive place, unjust and dangerous. He was much braver than I was, I thought. He asked me where I was. I told him. He said he was coming to meet me. When I woke up I felt excited and scared but then it seemed only a dream, not real, and I thought my desire to know my brother, to remember and to recover him, were generating these fantasies. At the time I was working for a gallery owned by a rich couple who sold the frozen ripples of wisdom and menace and grace to other rich people who thought such wisdom and menace and grace could be transferred to them through ritual and objects. These rich people might have been correct, but I began to feel guilty. I knew I'd been hired as much for my knowledge about painting as for my only partly unintentionally stylish gestures and wardrobe, which, despite much effort to acquire them outright, could only be purchased by the rich indirectly, through my labors. Underneath I knew the situation was grotesque despite the very smart people

involved, despite the sad-eyed sculptors and the entertainingly
wicked painters, despite the witty and cynical-but-kind critics.
Nonetheless I knew that it was a 100% sham. And I thought of
my brother fighting god knows what over land and sea and air to
come find me, and I thought if he finds me in this corrupt state,
he'll either turn right around and go back or, worse, his heart
will be broken and he'll evaporate in front of my eyes. I went
back and forth thinking this was foolish and a self-destructive
mirage to thinking this was the truth and a prophecy for enlightenment. I kept thinking that he'd come, that he'd *already*
arrived—and was watching me and waiting and judging and
hoping. It's probably true that the banal or indecisive are the
most culpable. The banal for their lack of drama when acquiesc-
ing to the insidious but obvious corruption. And the indecisive
for their inability to choose good over evil, for their inability to
decide which is which. I'm saying I stayed where I was. For the
moment. I didn't quit. In fact I enjoyed myself, the proximity to
not just the luxuries or to their absolutely righteous judgments
of taste but also to true beauty, the perfect accord of color and
manner and tone. But also at night before sleep and in the morning before getting out of bed I vowed to leave it. I told myself
that the greed and self-satisfaction and vanity defiled whatever
grace and momentary perfection was found there, and I promised
myself that I therefore had to leave and find another line of work
and what's more prepare for the arrival of my brother, whom
I thought would not so much purposefully sit in judgment of
me as he would helplessly compare what he had held dear and

protected throughout his trials with what I had relinquished without even being asked. But then, as I entered the action of the day, as I went about creating and fulfilling obligations, I thought the indecisive were like the blessed meek, that they made no evil and they made no justice, no good or bad. And the banal was simply another name for the everyday and another name also for those—the most of us or the all of us—who just float the direction of the current, who have no choice one way or another. And my days and nights would sway between these twin poles, toggle between these dialectical ways, a movement based on the hour and my mood. Sometimes I was tortured by the constant revolutions but more so I became slow and clouded. I lived in a sleepy daze… One day as I was leaving work a man came up to me. He said, 'Allow me to introduce myself. I'm your twin brother. Will you have dinner with me?' This man was of one race and I am of another so it was immediately clear that what he was saying was impossible. And yet his presence was enacting the very moment I'd been anticipating so I agreed to have dinner with him. He took me to a nearby restaurant where we both declined to order off the menu and each only took a glass of wine.

"The man who claimed to be my brother said, 'Fip mek dolly wolly! *A man who has had a bad childhood beats his dog in the park.* Now, I thought, we were finally getting somewhere. *You and I as a man beating a dog is the same as two supernovas eating each other elsewhere, which I don't mean symbolically and when you die you just die.* I came to believe in the profit motive and in the limited compulsions of our race and in the efficient distributive forces of capitalism. *You cannot be pure; you cannot be defiled.* I was until recently a systems engineer—do you know what that is? *There is no need to suffer on my account.* Sometimes it's a sweeping line, sometimes just a dot or a cramped squiggle. *I'm a ghost reborn a figure to tell you something an apparition in a room thirteen lines in a novel.* I was wandering the library, searching and not searching, a question permanently on my lips, growing hopeless. *All the signs tell you, and what's more I'm telling you, to feel the earth revolving under your feet, to listen to your lungs as you breathe and to vomit without shame.* And, we say to one another, if this is truly the case, says I to my maid or my maid to me, then perhaps it is not a jail at all and we are actually in the paradise the state had long-ago promised and in truth has fulfilled, despite our ignorance—and we moreover suffer continuously and unnecessarily out of pride and foolish apostasy. *I've committed suicide so you don't have to.* For any of the faces in the crowd or the phantoms that pass through my bedroom or that lie with me on the bed or any of those spirits somewhere else in the house. *I'm back from the dead so forgive me if I sound insane.* But then what do we do with the facts? *I've put your painting out in the sun and the canvas is warm.*'

"When this man who claimed to be my brother stopped speaking I excused myself to go to the bathroom. When I came back he was gone and our table had been cleared so I walked out. I thought he was a madman but I was disappointed he was gone and wanted to see him again—but I never did. Instead, I soon after quit my job at the gallery and got another better-paying one at an office. I'd decided to become rich myself so on my off days I began to take classes to become a real estate agent."

Oon had by this time finished his lemonade and put away his book. We got up and continued our walk through the park.

He said to me, "I love you."

I said to him, "I love you too so what."

Then a few minutes later he said, "On July 22nd, 2011, I met my friend Christopher for breakfast at a diner near my apartment. It was a hot day, the hottest day that summer so far and in fact one of the hottest ever on record. I asked Christopher some questions about tax accounting, which he answered very testily because he often gets testy when discussing money, of which he has had—but not currently, thus the testiness—a very great deal. In fact he was interested in figuring out a cheap but romantic place to stay in Vermont. The reason for this was he was arranging a rendezvous with a woman who lived in Maine and who for some reason wanted to meet him in Vermont. At this time Christopher was rather poor, but he still wanted to impress the woman. Since I'd been, very much coincidentally, also planning a vacation to Vermont at that time (Vermont is one of a handful of states that prohibits billboards), I said he could come back to my apartment and look through some of the travel books I'd recently collected. We finished our breakfast and made our way to my four-story walkup. The heat was a soup we plunged through. Back at my place, while Christopher used my bathroom, I arranged my tourist books on the kitchen table and also placed there a microwaved cup of hot coffee because even through it was sweltering, Christopher is an undeterrable drinker of hot coffee. He came out of the bathroom and started looking at the books. I had some dishes in the sink I needed to wash so I began and finished them. While doing the dishes I realized I was annoyed at Chris for his testiness. However I didn't want to give expression to the annoyance because I didn't see any purpose in arguing with him. Instead I decided to leave. I told him to just lock up when he'd finished with the books. He agreed and I left. My plan had been to go to the library and work on the ending to this performance about twins I was having trouble with. The rest was done but the ending didn't seem to be coming together and was causing me a great deal of frustration. I really didn't think a coda was necessary to the parts that had come before but on the other hand it seemed to finish rather bluntly without one. I thought having the work just fall into silence might be wrong but I thought having an addition might also be a mistake. I'd been going back and forth about this for weeks. It was a painful but typical predicament. I didn't want to distract from or dilute the stories that had come before, but I thought maybe without some bit at the end, some casting off, the careful order would, like a piece of knitting, nonetheless unravel. At the last moment on the way to the library instead of going to the library I went to the museum. By this time, I had completely forgotten about Christopher, Vermont, tax accounting, hot coffee and my annoyance, and I was only thinking about us—you and me, Oon and Noona—and about our walks and our brothers and sisters. I made a hurried tour of the museum. A Belgian conceptual artist was having a show there. For a time I distracted myself watching this artist lead sheep in a circle, chase tornadoes and carry a loaded gun through city streets. Then, having an idea, I sat in one of some chairs I'd found near stairs and wrote down a possible ending to my performance concerning these siblings. From that moment in the chair, my mistake or my silence—I still wasn't sure which, and in any case they operated and existed entirely independent of my desires, and maybe it was both of them—pulsed back and forth so as to surround and pervade each act of these strange twins."

Eugene Lim is the author of the novel *Fog & Car*. He runs Ellipsis Press, works as a librarian in a high school, and lives in Queens, New York.

*The Strangers* is printed and bound in an edition of one thousand copies at Thomson-Shore Printers. The text is composed in Fournier. Cyclone, a display by Hoefler & Frere-Jones, appears on the front cover. The photograph on page 213 was taken by the author.